~~Average~~ { Vegan } Teen

~~Average~~
{ Vegan }
Teen

By Christen Mailler

Vegan Publishers
Danvers, Massachusetts
www.veganpublishers.com

© 2023 by Christen Mailler

All rights reserved. No portion of this book may be used or reproduced in any manner whatsoever, without written permission, except in critical articles and reviews. For more information, please contact the publisher directly.

Design & typesetting by REBELCO

ISBN: 978-1-940184-70-8

Table of Contents

Part One

1. The Edge 1
2. Triangles 9
3. Last Supper 15
4. Friends First 19
5. Natural Disaster 27
6. Shadow of a Mother 35
7. Worthless Matches 43
8. Life Goes On 49
9. The Many Secrets of Six 55

Part Two

10. It Is True 63
11. Hard to Explain 67
12. Writing and Weeding 73
13. Mihku 79
14. Sippy 85
15. Big Noises 93

16.	The Life of a Squirrel	101
17.	Ruth	107
18.	Wild Jellyfish	115
19.	Fun Guy	125
20.	Lola	131
21.	Moxie	137
22.	A Lit Match	145
23.	Small Details	151

Part Three

24.	The Most Beautiful Sound	163
25.	Channel Five News	171
26.	The Whole Shebang	177
27.	Bucky	187
28.	Subtle Pressure	193
29.	Millie	199
30.	A Parallel Universe	207
31.	Ashes	213
32.	Maybe	221
33.	Dark Sunshine	227
34.	Wind	233

Part One

Chapter 1: The Edge

Kessa held her breath, as she always did, when Toria got to the little toenail. There wasn't much of a nail, and it was hard to paint it without getting some on the skin, though Toria always did an expert job. She ran her thumbnail along the base of Kessa's cuticle to scrape away the excess and then cleaned her own fingernails with a cotton ball soaked with polish remover. The acrid but familiar smell of acetone filled the room.

"What if a really cute boy who wasn't vegan asked you out? Would you go out with him?" Toria was now leaning forward to look in the mirror, tilting her head side to side and pushing her lips out like she always did when checking out her reflection or posing for a selfie. She was full of what-ifs about boys lately.

"It doesn't matter. I don't even know any boys interesting enough to consider, and neither do you."

"We will, though, soon." Toria lifted her chin and repositioned the clasp of her delicate silver chain so it was behind her neck. "So, would you? Would you date a non-vegan boy? What if he was vegetarian?"

"Vegetarian? I don't know. It depends. What if he wanted to kiss me?"

Reflected in the mirror, Toria rolled her eyes as she rearranged the perfumes, polishes, and makeup on top of the dresser. "Exactly—what if! You need to start thinking about these things, Kessa. Be prepared." She dabbed something pink onto her wrist and considered it for a moment, then shook her head, wiping the smudge off with her thumb.

There weren't any vegan boys or girls in their grade aside from Kessa. If there were, she would know, because she'd been with most of her peers since kindergarten, when she and Toria had met and become best friends.

In fourth grade, there had been that one vegetarian boy, a quiet, sandy-haired kid who never said much and ended up moving away the next year. She could still remember his lunches: they were always packed in a metal bento box and never had any dairy. At first, Kessa thought he might be vegan like her, but once, she caught a glimpse of an egg.

"Are you going to eat that?" she asked, half hoping he would come to his senses or that the egg was a mistake.

"Why?" he asked. "Do you want it? I'll trade for your applesauce."

"No," she had said, sliding the cup of applesauce closer to her bag. Hers was a plain lunch, but at least it didn't contain anything that had come from an animal's behind. She didn't say that to him, though. That would have been rude.

As far as she knew, she was still the only vegan in the whole school.

In any case, the boys in her class this year didn't exactly inspire any crush-like feelings, but maybe there would be one for her in middle school. A nice vegan boy, who liked animals and also didn't eat them. Yes, maybe next year she would have a crush on someone and Toria would finally be happy with her.

"You're right," Kessa said. "I bet there will be more options in middle school." She stared at the carpet, imagining herself small and buried in its light purple fibers, soft and grounded for all eternity.

"There will be." Toria nodded resolutely, her large brown eyes fixed on her reflection. "A whole new pool to choose from. Seventh graders like us, of course"—she turned to Kessa with a glossy grin stretching across the slight gap between her two front teeth—"and eighth graders! And don't you think junior high sounds sooo much more mature than middle school?"

A squiggly feeling thrashed around in Kessa's stomach. Toria was rushing everything. Kessa didn't need more boys to choose from; she didn't even care about the ones she already knew. Why was Toria so eager for everything to change when there was nothing wrong with the way things were?

Last year, Toria had told her mom to put her dollhouse in the basement and save it for her little sister, Audrina. It was a statement, a declaration that told the world that she wasn't little anymore. It was a power move in the puberty Olympics, and Toria was headed for gold. When the edge in her personality had first started to emerge, Toria had taken pastels to the pink walls of her bedroom and drawn roses with thorns, zodiac symbols, and cartoonish eyes with spiky lashes and dripping teardrops, a tattoo artist gone mad.

It was a cruel sort of thing to do to walls so perfect, walls that had never asked for a redo. Toria had the kind of bedroom many girls could only dream about, with its coveted window seat, wall-to-wall plush lavender carpeting, and a canopy bed, just like the princesses in storybooks had. The dollhouse had been the perfect accessory, and now . . . Well, now it had no place there. It simply would not fit in.

Hundreds of little plastic dolls with big heads and large eyes—the ones that were a surprise until you opened the package and had a weird smell—had once made their home in that dollhouse. In first and second grade, every girl had at least a few of them. The best part was, if Toria was in the right mood, she would just give her dolls away. Kessa still had the ones that Toria had given her, the rejects. Sometimes she took them out of her closet, just to look at them and change their outfits.

Toria sat down on the carpet, her gaze drifting up and down Kessa's bare legs. "Oh wow, you really need to shave."

Kessa drew her knees up closer to her chest and eyed Toria's smooth calves. She didn't really want to shave, because she knew that once you started, you would always have to do it, forever, otherwise the hairs would grow back all stiff and prickly. It seemed like a lot of work, and showers already had too many steps. In addition to the shampoo and conditioner and body wash she already used, her mom had given her special soap to stop pimples from making connect-the-dot puzzles all over her forehead.

Her mom had also bought her a deodorant crystal to rub under her armpits after showering. "This will help," she had said. Before sixth grade, Kessa hadn't thought she needed "help" with her smell, and she didn't really care about having a few pimples, but everyone, including her friend Maddy, who never wore makeup, made it pretty clear—she was supposed to care.

Even if Toria was only trying to help, it seemed an odd thing to do, to pressure your best friend into taking a sharp razor to her skin. But Toria could be a sharp person sometimes. Maybe that was the secret behind having an edge—cut through and stand out.

"Yeah, my mom is going to get me a razor. I'll try it right before I leave for the lake. I just don't want to go through the last week of school with my legs all slashed up."

"It's easy. You'll get the hang of it." Toria unscrewed the top of a small red pot of lip gloss and applied it with her pinkie. "You want some?"

Kessa got a whiff of the pungent, medicinal cherry scent and shook her head. The stuff was gooey and disgusting. Besides, they had work to do. Their end-of-the-year project was to assemble a collage based on any one of the books they had read as a class that year. No words or letters allowed. Their teacher, Mr. Brady, had provided magazines to cut images out of, but they were difficult to work with.

"How am I supposed to make a collage about Black Beauty with this?" Kessa held up a picture of a blender beside a bowl of fruit sitting atop a pristine kitchen counter. Even after flipping through her third South Shore Home and Living magazine, she had yet to find anything remotely horse related. The feature spread was titled "Transforming Your Outdoor Space with Perennials." Kessa wished this could have been a writing assignment instead. "The kids who picked The Secret Garden are going to have it so easy. What book are you doing?"

"The Diary of a Young Girl." Toria slid a large piece of poster board out from behind her dresser, and Kessa braced herself for the feeling that was bound to come.

She'd written about this feeling once for a class assignment, and she wasn't sure it had a name, but she called it "the Burn." It happened when someone had a lot of goodness in their life, but the Burn didn't hurt because you wanted that goodness for yourself—it only singed if you didn't think the person deserved the goodness. The injustice of it ate at you, like the tiniest bit of fire licking away at some lost and vulnerable part inside you. The Burn could come on when someone who was mean also happened to be really pretty, because mean people shouldn't get to be pretty. And sometimes the Burn would sneak up on you when a person seemed to have too many blessings for one body to hold.

Kessa didn't want to feel the Burn because of Toria, but sometimes the flames would just get at her and there wasn't a thing she could do about it. Toria had a lot of blessings. Not only was she beautiful, but she also had the best room Kessa had ever seen, the newest, most expensive type of phone, the most nail polish, and of course the most fashionable clothes. Toria had a lot of bests and mosts, and to top it all off, she was also artistic.

Toria was always being praised for the least little thing she scratched out. Half the class would crowd around just to watch her draw an outline of Hello Kitty. It never seemed fair, Kessa thought, because she wrote stories that were just as colorful and detailed as Toria's pictures, but nobody ever clapped for stories, and nobody ever oohed or aahed over a paper full of words.

"Ta-da!" Toria whipped around the poster and held it up in front of her chest, looking like one of the playing cards from Alice in Wonderland. Kessa bit down on her thumbnail. It was good, really good. There were better ways to describe it, for sure, but she didn't want to dwell on it.

Rather than clipping out whole images and gluing them down near each other, Toria had ripped up little bits of magazine paper in all different colors and assembled them into a complete portrait of Anne Frank.

"Okay, so that's an A plus!" Kessa said, wondering how the hundreds of shredded colored pieces had come together to make up such a realistic-looking face.

Toria shrugged and placed the poster next to a stack of half-cut-up magazines. "I'm getting pretty tired of doing this. It's going to take a while to finish the background in this same style."

The excessive talent was causing her some boredom? Poor Toria. No, Kessa thought, struggling to smother the Burn. It was important to be happy for friends—like Maddy was. She was always nice to people, even if they were undeserving. Like the time Lilyette Lane had made fun of Maddy's bathing suit after Maddy had invited her to her birthday pool party. Lilyette ignored her all day and did perfect backflips off the diving board, which everyone thought was amazing, and even Maddy applauded for her. She didn't even get Maddy a gift, and Maddy was still nice to her at school the next day, like nothing had even happened.

"It's really amazing," Kessa said, her face growing hot. "It's clever too. I bet no one else in the class will do it that way."

She frowned at her own collage, which was mostly blank with only a few glued-down images surrounded by vast poster-paper whiteness. Negative space. She opened another magazine and flipped through it, then paused on a page that caught her eye: a picture of an old-fashioned doll, the kind with a porcelain face and a frilly dress. The doll had lots of itchy-looking lace creeping up around its neck, and its glassy blue eyes stared out at her. Kessa scrolled her mind for adjectives, flipping through the thesaurus in her head. The lips were obvious rosebud perfection, but the doll's eyes were beautiful in a different way, a strange way. She liked it. Haunting. That was it.

Toria leaned forward to see the page, her eyes sharpened with dark black liner, the edge rolling off her tongue.

"Whoa, creepy. I mean, that is, literally, the creepiest thing I have ever seen."

Chapter 2: Triangles

A fly buzzed passed Kessa's face as she surveyed the lunch crowd and headed for the nearest open table, her damp T-shirt sticking beneath her backpack. It was one of those summer-is-coming days at the end of the school year that made bodies itch and thighs prickle with moist heat against the desk chairs. Perfume and sweat infused the air, hovering like a cloying smog above the apathetic slap of flip-flops and sandals.

"This is so unfair. Did you know they have A/C in the office? It's a legit icebox in there," Toria complained, adjusting one of her silver hoop earrings as they plopped down at the lunch table with Maddy. She side-eyed the group of boys cheering and high-fiving each other a few rows away.

"I know, right? I'm melting," Maddy said. She picked the cheese off a limp slice of school pizza.

Maddy had joined their school last year in fifth grade but had become instant friends with Toria when they had bonded one day over a mutual dislike of the school's music teacher. Mrs. Pascoe had a reputation for being mean and strict, even with the kindergartners.

"What kind of teacher yells at little kids?" Maddy had exclaimed as she passed the music room, which was filled with trembling five-year-olds who were being scolded for not singing correctly.

Toria had chimed back, "If you think that's bad, wait till you meet Mrs. Hungar, the school librarian. Don't breathe too loudly or she'll eat you alive!"

And just like that, Maddy laughed and joined them on the way to the girls' bathroom. It was easy for Toria to make friends, a little too easy. The thought caused worries about next year to swarm around in Kessa's head like a cloud of gnats, impossible to swat away.

From then on, it was no longer just Toria and Kessa—or Toressa, as they had once called themselves—but Toria, Kessa, and Maddy. A group of three. She never liked triangles, but now she was a part of two of them: one with her friends and one with her family. Her parents could have stayed together and granted her a sibling, making them a nice, even square. But she didn't do that daydream anymore.

Maddy pushed her pizza away and opened a carton of chocolate milk. "Hey, what's the matter with you, Kess? You okay? You look thirsty. Do you want my orange juice?" Maddy slid the mini-sized school carton of orange juice across the table toward Kessa.

"No thanks. I'm just kind of sad about leaving next week. What am I going to do without you guys?"

Toria put down her sandwich and raised her precise and manicured eyebrows. "Are you kidding me right now? You're spending the summer on a lake, and you're seriously going to complain about that? On a ridiculously hot day like today?"

Kessa groaned. "I know, but—"

Toria cut her off like she so often did, clipping Kessa's thoughts in half like a careless hairdresser. "Call me when you're working on your tan and then let me know how you feel. I think any of us would be happy to be lakeside all summer. Right, Maddy?" She looked to Maddy, who nodded, eyes widening in agreement.

"Anyway, I was going to say, my dad doesn't have internet at the house yet." He treated the lake house like an off-grid writing retreat. He said it was "Waldenesque."

"Wait—what? No internet? Still? I mean, isn't the entire world connected by now?" Toria said with the disdained tone of a spoiled princess in a poor village. "Not letting a kid have internet access is basically child abuse."

"Well, unlike some people," said Maddy, a smirk forming on her lips, "at least Kessa can survive without online beauty tutorials."

"It's not just beauty tutorials," Toria scoffed. "It's a whole beauty community. Besides, the two of you should be paying more attention. I really need to do your 'before' pictures, because once you see the light, you'll never go back. Trust me. You'll wonder why you waited so long."

Maddy shook her dark curly head like she was watching a Ping-Pong match. "There's no point in me wearing makeup. I'd just sweat it off during practice anyway. Who needs mascara melting in their eyes when trying to score a goal?"

Kessa had limited experience with face paint. Toria had once attacked her with a beauty blender, spackling her mottled skin smooth and filling in every pore. She had taken something pointy and wet to line Kessa's eyes in a shade called Midnight Kitten and applied a waxy rouge to her mouth. Afterward, the mirror, which Kessa had always trusted, held a startling new face, a sad Cleopatra with feline eyes and lips of wine red.

"Well, it's not an everyday look," Toria had said, touching up her cheekbones with gold shimmer. "I thought I'd glam you up a bit."

A while later, Kessa had rubbed her eyes without thought, and the mask had come away on her fingertips. Too afraid to confront the mirror again, she stepped right into the shower with washcloth in hand and scrubbed the mistake away.

No, makeup wasn't her thing, but nails were something else. The rules were simple, and once the polish was dry, you could dip your fingers into bags of chips and turn pages and scratch all your itches without care. Best of all, it was a way to feel pretty without changing your face.

"Will you guys promise to come over this weekend so we have some time together, just the three of us, before I have to go?" She held up the backs of her hands so Toria could observe the polish job that had been chipping away since last week's nail night.

Toria leaned forward on her elbows and laced her fingers beneath her chin. "What kind of friend would I be if I let you go off to the lake without a proper mani-pedi?"

"We'll be there," Maddy replied, balling up the grease-stained napkin from her pizza tray. "Hey, how were your report cards?"

"All As," Toria said breezily as she lifted her phone in front of her face. She held her two fingers out in a sideways peace sign and pushed out her lips.

"Ugh, please don't do the duck lips," Maddy groaned. "Anyway, I got mostly As and Bs. What about you, Kess?"

"Mostly average. You know, the usual Bs, but—"

"Well, I mean, honestly," Toria cut in, "if you didn't daydream through every other lesson, your grades would probably be a lot better."

"But," Kessa continued, "Mr. Brady said I should work on a new short story to enter into a writing contest. The entries are due at the end of the summer, and I'll have plenty of time." She gave a sharp exhale through her nose.

"That's awesome!" Maddy beamed at her. "Your writing is so beautiful. When he read that essay you wrote after spring break, I was, like, blown away. The whole thing sounded like poetry."

"Really? I was kind of embarrassed. I thought everyone looked bored."

"No, it was good. You really have a way with words. It did not sound like something a sixth grader wrote."

"Yeah, she's a regular walking thesaurus all right." Toria applied a shiny pink gloss to her lips and pressed them together with a small pop before reaching for her phone again. "Just because writing is flowery doesn't mean it's good, you know," she said, flicking her finger across the screen. "Ugh, I should have edited this one first. My eyes just aren't popping the way they should." She raised the phone in front of her face again and lifted her mascaraed lashes, holding her brown doe eyes unnaturally wide like a startled victim in a horror flick.

"You look nuttier than a fruitcake!" Maddy shrieked and threw her balled-up napkin across the table at Toria's tilted head. Toria didn't flinch.

Kessa opened the notes app on her phone where she kept track of all her ideas, and the table was quiet for a minute while everyone looked at their phones. She searched her mind for something to write, even the smallest spark of an idea, but when the bell rang, she was still staring at a blank space where all the words were supposed to be.

Chapter 3: Last Supper

Dinner was vegan macaroni and cheese. Homemade, not the boxed kind. Kessa made small piles with the cheesy noodles. Using her fork to drag bits of salad between the mountains, she paused to consider adding some extra dressing to create rivers, then leaned back in her chair to admire the new topography of her plate.

"Kessa?" Her mom's voice snapped her out of her distracted dining. "You're a bit old to be playing with your food. Is everything all right? You don't like it?"

"I'm just not that hungry." Kessa slouched in her chair, allowing her arms to fall loosely by her sides. "Why do I have to have my birthday at Dad's?"

"How many times do we need to discuss this? You know this is supposed to be your time with your dad." Her mom tucked an errant strand of wavy gray hair behind her ear and pressed her eyes closed for just a moment too long, lashes quivering, her typical show of irritation. The grooves on the sides of her mouth deepened as she frowned, wrapping down toward her chin like a marionette.

"Can't I just leave after my birthday? Just this once?" Kessa pleaded.

"It's only a couple of months, and you always end up having a great time. You'll get to hang out with Candice's children, Arthur and Millie. And their little sister—what's her name? Daisy? I bet she's walking and talking up a storm by now. Maybe you can babysit. Don't forget—you'll also be able to visit Ruth at the animal sanctuary. I know how much you look forward to that." Her mom shook her fork at Kessa as if to emphasize the point.

"But I'm still going to be away when I turn thirteen and..." Kessa hesitated for moment. "Things could... happen."

"Things? Like what?" Her mom moved her empty wineglass aside and leaned over her plate. "What do you mean?"

Kessa felt as if she were swelling like a balloon filling with water. The water had started dripping in the last week of school, slowly at first, but now it was getting too full, and she wasn't quite sure how to stop it.

"Mom, what if I get my period and there are no pads at the store and what if Dad has to"—Kessa lowered her voice to a harsh whisper—"buy them for me?" There was a lumpy feeling in her throat that always happened when she was about to cry but was trying not to.

"Oh goodness, honey, you don't have to worry about stores not having pads! I know rural Maine doesn't have much, but they do have basic feminine hygiene supplies. And I'll make sure you have stuff to take with you just in case." Her mom smiled and looked into her glass, tilting it from the stem as a little leftover bead of red rolled around like a single drop of blood.

Feminine hygiene supplies? Why did her mom have to talk like that? Kessa balled up her hands beneath the table. "It's honestly not that crazy for me to not want to start my period for the first time while stuck out in the middle of nowhere! There's still not even any internet there and I won't be able to go online and my friends will do fun summer stuff together without me and what if"—she choked back a sob—"and what if they become best friends together and don't want to hang out with me anymore when I come home?"

The balloon had not only filled up, it had burst, and she collapsed onto the table, burying her face in her folded arms. Without a word, her mom changed seats to take the chair next to her and began rubbing her back. The comforting scent of her mom's shampoo caused Kessa to let out another giant sob, her hot cheek growing damp against the tabletop.

"Oh, Kess." Her mom breathed out the words in a sympathetic exhale as she gathered up Kessa's hair and weaved it into a loose braid.

"It's not fair." Kessa sniffled. Her whole body shook with each inhale, but the sore lump pushing against her throat subsided. "Why can't I just stay here and hang out with my friends and go to camp and just have a regular summer and a fun birthday with my friends like a normal teenager?"

"Well, I know you're not quite thirteen yet, but you sure are behaving like a teenager already." Her mom slapped the table with her palm. "You know, when I was your age, I was emotional all the time. Cried at the drop of a hat. The hormones started kicking in and—"

"Mom," Kessa interrupted as she sat up in her seat, rolled her eyes to the ceiling, and took a deep breath. "Can't I just cry and vent without you making it about hormones and stuff?"

"Of course." She chuckled as she wrapped her arms around Kessa's shoulders and kissed her salty cheek before rising to meet the knocking on the front door. Kessa stretched the sleeve of her shirt over her hand and wiped at her face. Another reason not to wear makeup—at least there was nothing to smear.

Chapter 4: Friends First

"So, are you going to hang out with those weird kids who live by the lake?" Toria asked as she applied a coat of dark purple polish to Kessa's chewed-up nails.

"You mean Arthur and Millie? They're not that weird." Kessa watched attentively, biting her tongue as Toria used her long thumbnail to scrape away the little bit of polish that had pooled on the side of her nailbed.

"Aren't they homeschooled?" Maddy chimed in with an emphasis on the word home. "Remember that one girl, last year in fifth grade, with the super-long braid? Wasn't she homeschooled before then?"

Toria guffawed. "Rachel Feldsted? Um, yes! How could we ever forget? She was sooo awkward! And remember how she was obsessed with drawing those freaky half-human, half-horse people?"

"They're called centaurs," Kessa said flatly.

"Whatever. They looked ridiculous. I tried to show her how to draw a regular horse, but she refused to take any pointers. Hopeless."

Maddy hugged her knees and wiggled her freshly painted toenails. "So how long does this stuff take to dry?"

Kessa crossed the room to fetch the mini fan from her bureau. "Actually, Arthur and Mille aren't homeschooled—they're unschooled. It's different. They can do whatever they want. They don't have to learn anything . . . I mean, they do learn stuff, but it's just whatever they want to, whenever they feel like it."

"Okaaay, that is obviously not going to turn out well. How do they learn to read and write, and what about math? They just teach themselves?" Toria snorted. "They probably just watch TV all day. Can you imagine?" She blew a bubble with her gum and it made a loud snap.

"I don't know. I think it sounds kind of okay." Kessa clicked on the mini fan, and a burst of cool air whooshed up the hair around her face. "You get to follow your own interests and find what you're passionate about and then spend most of your time just doing that thing until there is something else that interests you. Of course, I've already decided to become a famous author, so I would spend all my time writing, naturally."

"Writing and daydreaming!" Maddy teased with a playful smirk.

"I'm planning to write a new story this summer." Kessa smiled into the breeze of the fan. "I'm going to bring my laptop with me and work on it while I'm at the lake. I'll be inspired there, like Thoreau. If it comes out good enough, I'll submit it to that contest Mr. Brady told me about. If I win, I'll be discovered. I could be famous."

"Like, honestly, it is possible," Toria said. "Unschooling could leave a lot of room for more interesting stuff. I could become a top beauty guru before I even get to college and then, you know"—she snapped her gum again and shook a bottle of blue nail polish—"explode onto the scene with my own makeup line. Maybe school is totally pointless. Maybe we're all just wasting our time and potential."

"Exactly." Kessa held her nails in front of the fan, feeling even more confident now that Toria was agreeing with her. "Plus,

Friends First

Arthur and Millie are really smart, especially Millie. She's young, but she reads lots of grown-up stuff, and she knows tons of big words that you wouldn't expect a little kid to know. It just goes to show, maybe school isn't everything."

"How about that boy, Arthur?" Toria said, cutting into the breeze and tapping Kessa's nail lightly to see if it was dry.

"Ew. No! He's just . . . he's just Arthur." Once, last summer, he had come back from a hike covered head to toe in mud and soaking wet, having been caught in a flash rainstorm while he was out. He had invited her to go on the hike, but she had said no and stayed inside doing a bead project with his little sister Millie instead. "I mean, I've known him my whole life. We've just been friends for so long . . ."

"That actually makes it doubly perfect for romance." Toria unscrewed the cap and tested the metallic blue on her long pinkie nail. "Everything is better if it starts out as a friendship. It's like, here's this guy who knows you so well and cares about you in a really real way, not about how you look or anything . . ." She trailed off with a wistful look and blew at her little finger.

"But what if you really like just being friends?" Maddy said. "If it becomes a romance, there's no going back, right? I mean, you could ruin the friendship forever if things don't work out." She leaned her dark curly head against the side of the bed, waiting for her turn with the fan.

Kessa lowered her hands and sang into the fan like an auto-tuned pop star. "Maddy makes a very good point, woo-hoo-ooh."

Maddy giggled and sang back to her, "I'm gonna miss you, Kessa Caliper, yeah-yeah, yeah."

Kessa spread her hands with their ten pretty purple tips, shiny and dry. New polish was the perfect antidote to anxiety nibbling. A nail biter's trick. "I'm going to miss both of you guys wicked bad. And my nails will not look this good again for months." She lowered her voice. "Not that it matters, since I'll be out in the—"

"—middle of nowhere!" Maddy and Toria mocked in unison before cracking up in a fit of giggles.

"Okay, okay, I get it. I just . . . you know, it's the whole summer." Kessa swallowed the beginnings of another sore lump. "And you guys will go to the pool"—her voice quivered—"and the mall." She took in a shaky breath, pressing her palms to her face.

"Nooo, no, honey, don't ruin your manicure. Aw, shush, Kessy girl, don't cry, don't cry." Despite her newfound edginess, Toria could be surprisingly maternal sometimes. You could never be sure when that side of her would come out, but when it did, everything about her felt safe, just like it had back when they were six and seven. When they could fit side by side in a bean bag chair and Toria would draw Kessa unicorns to color in during indoor recess and pull her underneath the umbrella when they waited for the bus in the rain. Kessa liked when Toria took care of her. All of that unpredictable sharpness fell away when Toria did nails, as steady and attentive as the polish was smooth.

"Come here, little bomboncito. It's okay. We love you." Toria scooted across the floor and wrapped her arms around Kessa, and then Maddy leaned in. It didn't make sense to hate triangles, Kessa realized. They were a sturdy shape—just three points to the most stable figure in the world.

"Oh, hey, Kess, I'm really sorry, but I think we have to get going soon." Maddy picked up her buzzing phone like it was something hot, trying not to smudge her nails. "It's my mom, and she's going to be here in ten."

"There's just one other thing." Kessa picked at the carpet fibers, twisting and tugging the fuzzy gray bits as she watched another teardrop plop down and soak in. "I'm still freaked that I might start my period while I'm there."

"Did you already pack pads? Because if you plan on swimming at the lake, you're really going to want one of these." Toria, who had already had her period for a full two years, pulled a plastic-wrapped tube from her purse and pretended to smoke it like a cigar. She bit down on the tampon with the corner of her mouth and gave an exaggerated wink.

"Ahhhhh!" Maddy screeched, clapping her hands together. "Remember when someone left a bloody pad floating in the water at my pool party last year and my mom had to fish it out with a net?"

"I bet it was Lilyette's! It probably came loose after one of those ridiculous backflips." Toria let out a loud cackle and the tampon fell from her mouth.

Recalling the incident sent them all into a full-blown laughing fit. They didn't easily recover from these, because once they got going, it was almost impossible to stop before their ribs got sore.

Kessa caught herself in the mirror. She was puffy and red, her hair sticking to her blotchy cheeks by the damp tracks of tears. All the makeup in the world couldn't have fixed it, but at least it was still her own, familiar face. "Guys, look at me! I am such a mess!" Maddy fell back onto the floor, still giggling, as Toria took another pretend drag from her pink-and-purple "cigar."

"We are still definitely going to talk this summer. You know that, right?" Toria said, taking on a razorless tone as she slid the tampon back into her purse.

"And you can call us anytime," Maddy chimed in.

"On my birthday for sure." Kessa took a deep breath as she used the bottom of her shirt to dry her eyes.

"For sure," Toria repeated, reaching for Kessa's hand. "Oh, I am good," she cooed, followed by a low whistle. "You're nails look ah-mazing."

. . .

"Yes, Mom. I've got everything. I have my phone, my computer, my chargers, my summer reading, and all the important things. I double- and triple-checked."

"Are you going to bring Chuck Chuck?" her mom asked, sitting down on the end of the bed and surveying the suitcases and duffel bags that covered the floor.

Kessa had a stuffed woodchuck that she used to carry around when she was little. But Chuck Chuck was extremely worn and tattered, and though it had spent every night in bed with Kessa since she was a baby, it was time to leave the stuffed animal at home. She was going to be thirteen soon. It was a grown-up thing to do, she had decided, to not bring Chuck Chuck.

"No, not this year. I'm nearly thirteen. I don't need to bring my lovey on every trip." But even as she said it, she felt a pang of guilt. She had placed Chuck Chuck on top of her bookcase to try to transition away from sleeping with her every night. Kessa cast a glance at Chuck Chuck, looking all soft and saggy and very huggable way up there on the top shelf, and hoped her feelings wouldn't be hurt. Some of her dad's books were on that shelf too. They weren't books she was interested in reading... yet. But she was very proud to display them. After all, not everyone had a famous author for a dad. "Mom, if Dad wasn't a writer, do you think he would want to spend his summers in a boring old town, cut off from everything and everyone?"

"Well, your dad has always liked to have his quiet. He can't write if there are distractions. Even when we were married, I would go whole days hardly seeing him at all, and we lived together." She scoffed. "He would hole up in the attic study and not come out for hours at a time."

"Were you friends first? I mean, before you started dating?"

"We sure were, and I'm proud to say we still are. You know, some parents don't have a good relationship after divorce."

"I know. I just wish he could have a summer home that was a little closer to Rhode Island. I get that it's a good place for him to write, but really, it's probably the worst place for someone like me, or for anyone my age."

"Now, why would you say that? You have that writing contest coming up, and this will be the perfect time to work on your story. I thought you wanted to be like Thoreau." She smiled wryly and patted the covers over Kessa's legs.

"Well, I do," Kessa said, "but what most people don't realize is that he actually had access to a constant stream of visitors and wasn't nearly as isolated as everyone thinks. Walden was a popular pond near a main road, and Concord, Massachusetts, wasn't that far from Boston. If he had really wanted isolation, he would have chosen Lake Wabanaki."

Chapter 5: Natural Disaster

Nestled into the writing nook in the room off the front hall of the lake house, Kessa clicked her old clunky laptop shut. She was distracted from her new story by a pang of loneliness and longing, a feeling she couldn't place. It wasn't supposed to be like this. The first few days at the lake were usually filled with all the things she couldn't wait to do—reading beneath the sunrise, diving off the dock, taking out the canoe, and of course, throwing her arms around her dad, his softness as welcome as her quilted mattress up on the second floor.

Several unvarnished bookcases lined the walls, each loaded with books. The dim room had dark-brown fake-wood wall paneling that her dad said was left over from the 1960s. Kessa's mood sagged like the middle of the largest bookcase, which was weighted down by horizontally stacked tomes that were too tall to fit in neat vertical rows. Was this how she was going to feel all summer? She wrapped her arms across her stomach. The pain moved deeper, a dull gnawing that might possibly be soothed by a snack.

Her dad had made her a tofu scramble for breakfast . . . Well, he had attempted it, anyway. She had tried to be nice and eat it all, but it was kind of a chore to choke it down. Her mom would have used turmeric to make it look yellow and lots of onion powder and garlic salt to give it some flavor, and she would have fried it all up in a pan with oil, getting it nice and toasted. Her dad's style of tofu scramble was just a block of tofu cooked in the microwave and mashed with a fork.

Now, she needed something more satisfying to calm her appetite. Cookies might do the trick, but she wasn't sure if there'd be any left, because her dad ate them faster than she could. On her way to raid the kitchen, Kessa stopped in the living room to greet Bucky.

"Hey there, Buckster, what should we do?" she said. The old beagle lay curled up on the couch and looked at her with his teary amber eyes. "I wish you could tell me what you're thinking." Kessa stroked the large, faded salt-and-pepper spot of fur on his back. Bucky plopped his chin back down on the couch. "Don't you ever get tired of just lying around all day? I miss when you used to want to go out and play." He closed his eyes and flicked his tail as she ran her palm along his coat.

When Kessa was younger, he had been more energetic, constantly pressing his nose to the screen door with a quivering tail, begging to meet the sun and the grass and the line where the sand met the lake. She loved the way the water teased at his paws and the way he jiggled the wetness from his coat.

Her dad had adopted Bucky when she was two years old and had originally named him Lucky. As a toddler, Kessa couldn't say the L sound, so she called him Bucky instead, and the name just stuck. But, back then, she also called him a bagel instead of a beagle.

She kissed the top of his head, and his ears twitched beneath her chin as they perked up at the squeak and creak of footsteps coming down the stairs.

"My two loves!" her dad said as he came into the room. "Are you having a nice conversation?" He nodded at Bucky on the couch and gave him a rub on the head. "I love these ears," he cooed in his doggy baby talk as he scratched around Bucky's neck. Bucky's tongue spilled out and he thumped his tail, soaking up the attention like a thirsty mop.

"He's not very active anymore." Kessa loosened her ponytail, a familiar ache tugging at her temples. She ran her fingernails along her sore scalp and melted back into the couch. Bucky's laziness was rubbing off on her.

"And neither are you!" her dad exclaimed. He put his hands on his hips and turned toward the window. "You're usually so busy I can barely get you in here to eat lunch! You'd be out on the canoe, doing your nature projects in the yard, reading in the hammock out front, or running around with Arthur and Millie. Why don't you go see what they're up to?"

"I just want to hang out with Maddy and Toria."

"Kessa, just go outside. Look—it's a gorgeous day. There's no need to mope around like ole Bucky here." He unlatched the window and slid it up. Fresh air filled the room with the wonderful scent of early summer. "Lake Wabanaki is as close as it gets to paradise! I'm going to grab a bite right now and then go write for a few more hours. Let's take the canoe out later after lunch. How 'bout it?"

"Okay," Kessa said with a sigh. "I guess I'll call over to Arthur and Millie's and see if they want to come over."

• • •

"So, are you still vegan?" Arthur didn't look up as he spoke; he was focused on drawing a compass in the sandy dirt with a long stick. His dark hair had a habit of falling in front of his face, which caused him to periodically jerk his head back in an effort to toss the bangs from his eyes.

Kessa scrunched up her face. "You ask me that every single year. Yes, I'm still vegan. It's not just a diet, okay? It's a way of life."

"Whoa, sorry. I was just asking is all." Arthur gestured to his drawing on the ground. "Maybe we should use this to set up orienteering points around the lake—make a treasure hunt or something."

"How is a silly drawing on the ground supposed to help us with anything?" She hung her leg over the side of the hammock and pushed her foot into the dirt to get a good swing going. She tried to think of what Toria would say. Kessa wasn't fluent in that sweet but sharp language that flattered and cut at the same time, when words of heat and ice melted together on the tongue. "I'm too old to play treasure hunt. Besides, shouldn't you be babysitting Daisy?"

Arthur scoffed. "I'm older than you. And don't act like a treasure hunt is all babyish. You liked it last year." He shrugged and threw the stick down into the dirt. "Anyway, Daisy fell asleep on the couch, so we have at least an hour. Do you want to go for a swim?"

"It's not hot enough yet, and I don't feel like it." Kessa pulled out her phone and scrolled through the photo album. There were loads of pictures of her and Toria and Maddy acting goofy and making silly faces. "Honestly? I really don't even want to be here right now."

"Yeah, we can tell," Millie chirped from high up in the tree. As usual, she had her nose buried in a book. Arthur said she had learned how to read on her own when she was about three. Last summer, she had taught herself French with a bunch of lessons on discs she borrowed from the library in town. She was only nine. Kessa looked up into the tree and saw a patch of bright frizzy red hair, a burst of fire among the leaves and branches.

"I think you need an attitude adjustment—absolument!" Millie plucked a broad leaf off the branch she was sitting on and sent it sailing down to the hammock. "Delivery!"

Kessa caught the leaf and waved it back and forth in front of her face, tracing over its veiny pathways with her eyes. "I know, guys. I'm sorry I'm being such a downer. I actually did kind of miss you," she said with a half smile. "Plus, if it weren't for you two, I would have nobody to celebrate my birthday with every summer."

"So that's all we are to you, huh? Just a couple of birthday guest stand-ins?" Arthur shot her a contemptuous glare.

"No." Kessa pushed herself up in the hammock. She was caught off guard by the note of hurt in his voice. "No, that's not what I meant. I honestly don't know what I would do without the both of you. You're my best friends out here on the lake. I'm sorry I'm in a mood. You just don't understand what I'm missing out on back home by being here this summer."

"Missing out? You mean on stuff like this?" Arthur said, grabbing her hand and eyeing the purple polish on her nails.

"Hey, excuse you!" She yanked her hand away, suppressing a smile and savoring the aftertaste of sass that lingered on her lips.

"What? I like it. I like it." Arthur backed away with his hands in the air and looked up at Millie. "Hey, Snack Attack, are you hungry yet?"

"Please don't call me that, and yes, I am." Millie wedged her book under her armpit and began climbing down from the tree. A branch caught on her faded and stained T-shirt, causing it to rip. "Dang it! Now I'm going to have to sew that."

Arthur laughed. "Oh, come on, Mill, you love to sew."

"That is true." She jumped from the lowest branch, which was still pretty high up, and as she put her arms out for the landing, her book fell to the ground.

"What are you reading there, little Millipede?" Kessa hopped out of the hammock and stooped to pick up the dog-eared paperback. Millie swooped in and snatched it up like a diving seagull, but not before Kessa caught a glimpse of the cover: a man and a woman stood clinging to each other on the beach, a saturated sunset casting a heated glow across their faces. The woman's cheek was pressed up against the man's chest, and she clutched her torn clothing as if it would be blown away any minute by the same wind that swept up her hair in frenzied golden swirls.

Millie's pale cheeks flushed to match her hair. "It's nothing!" She tucked the book back under her arm and marched toward her and Arthur's house like a soldier on a mission.

Kessa clapped a hand over her mouth and raised her eyebrows at Arthur. "She's allowed to read that stuff? Those books have, you know"—she lowered her voice—"adult content."

Arthur shrugged. "Eh, we can read whatever we want."

"Well, I can too. I just don't think I would pick a tacky romance novel. There's nothing interesting about that kind of writing. That's what my dad says, and he would know."

"So, because your dad is a writer, you get to decide what's worthwhile to read and what's not?"

Kessa opened her mouth to reply, but there were no words at the ready this time. This wasn't the Arthur she was used to. He stopped and put his hand against a tall tree, facing her like the gatekeeper of the woods that spread out in the distance behind him.

"Are you still writing stories?" he said, his tone a bit softer, like he really did care.

"Yes, but I'm kind of stuck right now on my current WIP."

"Work in progress?"

She didn't think he would know what that meant. "Yes. I'm writing a story for a contest. My teacher thinks I could win," she added smugly.

"Well, I have a great idea for a plot." Arthur dug the toe of his boot into the roots of the tree. His mouth was a straight line, yet by some slight quiver of the lip, she could tell he was smiling. "About a natural disaster. A thriller."

"Thanks, but I don't need any help. Besides, if it's such a great idea, then why don't you write it yourself?"

"Maybe I will." He ran his hand along the bark, eyeing it closely as if there were secrets hidden between the cracks, the straight line of his mouth breaking open a bit. "Are you going to come over with us? We have vegan snacks."

Kessa skipped up the stairs and stood on the front porch. "Maybe later. I need to get back to my writing." It sounded important and responsible. She could play and eat snacks like a child or work at the task of her future career. Real writers always prioritized their craft. She didn't leave Chuck Chuck behind for nothing. She needed to try to be more grown up this summer—after all, she was almost thirteen.

"Okay then." Arthur marched ahead a few paces and then turned back to look at her. "Kessa?" he called.

"What?"

"I once read somewhere that the first draft is just you telling yourself the story."

"You're giving me tips?" Kessa put her hand on her hip and cocked her head to the side, letting her limp brown hair fall like tangled ribbons over her right shoulder. She thought the pose might look cool, somewhat intimidating, somewhat edgy.

"Yeah. Why not?"

"Well, you just seem to think writing is really simple. And it's not." She turned on her heel and reached for the door handle, but as she stepped forward, she slid on some spilled water near Bucky's bowl and fell into an awkward split. If she hadn't worn her old flip-flops it probably never would have happened, but it did, and there was no graceful way to recover. Arthur was up the stairs in a flash, and she kept her head down so he wouldn't see the color creeping up her cheeks—some common rosy tint of humiliation, she was sure.

"Are you okay?"

She could feel his smile on her back as she pushed off with her hands and slid her legs properly beneath her. "I'm fine."

With the screen door safely shading her complexion, she watched him hop down the steps and jog away. She wondered what vegan snacks he had been referring to. Pretzels? Something better, maybe, like chips or cookies? Might they have assembled a fort in the living room after they ate or wandered back outside to discover hidden treasure in the backyard? It gave her a weird, lonely feeling to watch him leave. A feeling that nestled in the little hollow at the base of her throat. A feeling that couldn't just be swallowed away.

Chapter 6: Shadow of a Mother

The sky ripped open above the lake like it sometimes did, and once the rain started, it went on for days. Tuesday, Wednesday, and Thursday were spent hovering over puzzles, reading, writing, and watching television shows punctuated by endless, unskippable commercials. Not that it mattered what day it was—Wabanaki summers were never that defined. But Kessa was ready for the sun when it finally broke through early on Friday morning, sliding in through her curtains and splashing a bright line across her carpet like a familiar pathway.

Millie and Arthur met her on the dock for a swim. The rain had left the lake chilly, so Kessa was prepared to jump in, dunking fully under to bypass the shrieking stage. It could get pretty loud when the lake crept up into your armpits as you slowly lowered yourself in, but once your head was under, it was done.

Afterward, they lay themselves out like sardines in the sun. Millie slid her towel between Arthur's and Kessa's, and they settled onto their stomachs, breathing and shivering nose to nose until their backs warmed. Of course, it was midmorning, so it wasn't long before Millie suggested they all venture inside for snacks. Kessa threw her beach dress over her bathing suit and followed them through the woods that divided their properties until they came to the side yard. She curled her toes as the dirt and sand collected in her flip-flops and the tall grass tickled and itched against her calves until the faded blue siding of their house came into view.

Millie picked up an overturned stool and pushed it beneath the open window, parted the sheer curtains, and carefully climbed in. "Regarde ta tête!" she shouted over her shoulder.

Kessa watched, puzzled, as Arthur climbed up the stool, just as Millie had done. "Watch your head," he said.

"Can't we just use the front door?"

"No. Mom has it locked so Daisy can't get out, so we just go this way sometimes." Arthur ducked his head through the curtains.

Kessa straddled the windowsill and then swung her other leg around until both feet dangled against the inner wall like Humpty Dumpty. She surveyed the permanent disaster zone that Arthur and Millie referred to as the living room.

The thing about Arthur and Millie's house was that, like most of Millie's stained and raggedy shirts, it was not especially clean most of the time, and today things looked worse than Kessa had ever seen before. Piles of pillows and empty juice boxes were scattered around the room, and bits of firewood and soot from the hearth littered the floor. LEGO bricks and hair elastics were strewn all about. But the smell of old carpet and fireplace ash was the same as Kessa had remembered. If you stayed inside for a while, you would hardly notice it, but coming in from the fresh air was always a bit startling to the nose.

"Baby, no. Baby, no!" Daisy shouted, pulling a giant bowl of chips from the couch to the floor. She shrieked with delight and proceeded to jump in place, clapping her hands as she reveled in the crunch of potato chips beneath her feet.

Kessa watched, slightly alarmed, as Daisy, in nothing but a diaper, picked up the greasy chip bits from the shaggy brown carpet and proceeded to shove them into her mouth.

"Uh, your sister?" Kessa said as she gestured in Daisy's direction. "Should she be doing that?"

"Oh, that's toddlers for ya!" Millie shouted over her shoulder as she strolled ahead into the kitchen.

Arthur stuck his hands into the giant pile of LEGO pieces taking up the entire middle portion of the sofa. Several large, stained cushions were stacked in the corner beside the window, a tower that likely had to do with one of Millie's fort-building endeavors. Their couch hardly ever had all of its cushions on it at one time.

Daisy crawled underneath the coffee table and pressed her face against the underside of the glass top. It was smeared with fingerprints, and a variety of paint colors coated the splattered wooden frame. Kessa knelt down and peeked under the table. "Hi, Daisy."

"Hi, Dizzy," Daisy mimicked, opening and closing her hand, which looked like a small chubby starfish.

"It's me, Kessy. Remember?" Kessa looked into Daisy's almond-shaped gray eyes and held out her arms. "Do you want to come out of there?"

Daisy shook her head, and a little coil of strawberry-blonde hair fell between her brows. She pulled at her diaper and made a pouty face.

"Do you need a change?"

She nodded and began to stand up, but before Kessa could stop her, she slammed her head into the glass ceiling of the table and let out a long, slow wail like a lost captain languishing at sea.

Millie pranced around the corner and dove for her baby sister. "We told you not to go under there," she scolded. Daisy blinked through her tears and climbed into Millie's lap.

"Where is your mom?" Kessa asked.

"Candice? She's in the studio." Millie enveloped Daisy's tiny body in a hug and kissed her cheek.

Their mom, Candice, was an artist. She had graduated from a prestigious art school and sold her works in boutique beachside shops all across New England. Kessa didn't see her often during the summer since Candice was usually painting out back in the enclosed porch studio. Every now and then, she would emerge from her lair like Punxsutawney Phil. Covered in paint, she would rummage for food in the kitchen, only to quickly retreat once again to her artist's realm. Millie once joked that if Candice saw her shadow, she would make dinner that night. She never saw her shadow, of course, and she never did make dinner either. In that way and many others, as Kessa had come to know over the years, Candice was just a shadow of a mother. There, but not really.

Only, last year had been slightly different, when Daisy was smaller and Candice had spent many hours on the couch, holding her or nursing her to sleep with the curtains drawn, eating never-ending crunchy snacks from a wide silver bowl, her tired eyes bouncing and shimmering in the light of the TV. The studio was a black hole then. "Kids aren't allowed in there," she warned, but nobody wanted to go back there anyway. It was a hot den of turpentine and sun that you couldn't hide from.

Kessa rarely ever saw their dad because he traveled a lot for work. "That's the party line" was what Arthur said. She didn't know what he did, only that he appeared randomly throughout the summer weeks to mow the lawn or take their beat-up old boat out into the middle of the lake. Whenever he returned from a boat ride, he emitted a peculiar skunky smell, eyes glossy and distant, wavering like the horizon over a patch of hot tarmac.

• • •

"You will love this, Kessa!" Millie exclaimed as she lifted Daisy up onto the couch. "Hold on, I'll get it."

Millie emerged from the kitchen with a bowl of cookies and placed them in the center of the coffee table. "Oreos!" she said proudly. "They're vegan. I know, because you told us that last year, and I didn't believe you, remember? But I looked at the ingredients and, you're right, no animals or anything from them."

Kessa peered into the bowl. It was not just a few Oreos. Millie had dumped an entire package in there. "Wow, that's . . . a lot of cookies."

Millie beamed. "I know! There should be enough here for dinner too—as long as Candice doesn't get ahold of them."

Daisy scooted herself off the couch. "Cookie to Baby Dizzy. Yes!" she said, reaching for the bowl.

Kessa grabbed a cookie and headed into the kitchen to get some water. She had to poke around in the cabinet for a few minutes to find a glass to use. Most of the cups had some weird crud on them or a whitish film that didn't wash off very easily. Even though they owned a dishwasher, for some reason none of their dishes ever seemed very clean. She chose a jam jar and gave it a rinse in the sink before filling it from the tap. She was about to head back to the living room when Candice walked in through the open doorway on the side of the kitchen.

"Kessa!" Candice exclaimed. "It's so nice to see you. Is it really that time of year already?" She threw her arms out to embrace Kessa beneath the kitchen skylight, her many rings and bracelets glinting in the sun. "The spring just flew by, didn't it?" Daisy, upon hearing her mother's voice, toddled in across the sticky tiled floor. She held her arms up with a cookie in each hand. Candice pulled her hair, long and coarse as a horse's tail, to one side and scooped her up. "How's my Daisy Doo?"

Daisy patted the top of her curly tuft and scowled. "Dizzy Doo. Baby hurt."

"Oh," said Kessa, "she bumped her head under the coffee table a few minutes ago."

"For Pete's sake! She has got to stop doing that." Candice set Daisy down on the floor and peered into the fridge. Daisy ran back into the living room as Candice grabbed a can of beer and popped it open. It let out a sharp hiss. "Well, you know where I'll be if you kids need anything." She walked back to her studio with drink in hand, looking a lot thinner than Kessa had last seen her. "Oh, and if you wouldn't mind—change her diaper, please, when you get a chance."

"Your mom wants you to change Daisy's diaper," Kessa announced as she walked back into the living room and took a seat in an old rocking chair by the fireplace. She noticed an ancient wad of gum that had long ago glued itself to the curved wooden armrest and carefully placed her hands in her lap.

"I heard her ask you to do it," Millie replied, not bothering to look up from her book as she munched on an Oreo, cookie crumbles collecting in between the open pages.

"But she's not my sister—she's yours. You should do it."

"Why? Because I'm a woman? That's sexist, Kessa," Millie said with her mouth full. She shook out her book and sent a rain of crumbs sprinkling to the floor. "Why didn't you ask Arthur?"

"I'm not sexist!" Kessa hissed. "Arthur? Can't you do it?"

"Nah, I don't really like to do that." Arthur sat raking his hands thoughtfully through the giant pile of LEGO bricks.

Kessa leaned forward in the rocker and sighed at Daisy, who had just pulled out a long stick from the big brick fireplace. "Hey, Daze, I'm gonna change your diaper now, okay?" Daisy's soot-covered diaper was so full it was sagging between her legs. Kessa knelt down beside the hearth and tried to take the stick out of the toddler's grubby little hands.

Daisy let out an ear-piercing scream and ran out into the front hall, where she banged her bit of firewood on the screen door like a trapped victim in a burning building.

"Out! Out!" she shouted.

"Yeah, good idea," Millie said as she hopped off the couch and made a dash for the window.

"That reminds me, I'm working on something important out in the yard." Arthur grabbed a few more cookies before straddling a stack of cushions and following Millie through the curtains.

Kessa picked up a clean diaper from the open box at the base of the staircase and settled her eyes on Daisy, who had already given up on going outside and was back at the hearth pulling out more sticks and chucking them on the floor. As Daisy got busy scraping a sooty stick against the wall, Kessa pulled off the old wet diaper before helping her step into a new one.

"You're a natural at that." Kessa's head jerked up as Candice appeared, tall and willowy like some kind of spirit drawn from the slivery shafts of sunlight that slid between the broken kitchen blinds. She spied the bowl of cookies and picked it up, cradling the dish in her arms like a newborn. "You kids are all done with these, aren't you?"

"Yes. Thank you," Kessa replied as she stood up, holding the dirty diaper at arm's length. "What should I do with—"

"Ah! You can put them in the bag in the kitchen. There are wipes on the dining room table too—in case you get a messy one!" She laughed like they were long lost friends, bonding over an inside joke. Candice had always been like that. Her own words made her laugh even when no one else did, even when there was nothing to laugh about. "Just make sure the front door is always latched before you go out the window so our little Daisy doesn't escape."

Daisy toddled over to her and thrust her tiny hands up in the air. "Up. Up!"

"Not now, sweetie. Mommy's got to go paint." Candice placed a cookie into each of Daisy's outstretched hands. Daisy scrunched up her nose and hurled the cookies on the floor. She sat down on her bottom and wailed as tears streaked down her hot face like a sweating tea kettle.

"Mrs. . . . um." Kessa paused, catching herself before saying the family's last name because Candice didn't like to be called "Mrs." anything. "I mean, Candice? Perhaps Daisy would like to go outside for a bit? I can watch her. I don't mind. I think she really wants to go out and play."

"Oh, Kessa, you are an absolute angel!" Candice exclaimed. "Take her for as long as you want. She might get tired around two, in which case you can just lay her down for a nap here on the couch. She usually cuddles up with that old afghan there." She pointed to a colorful yarn blanket sprawled across the side of the sectional that still had cushions on it. She waltzed out of the room with the cookies, leaving Kessa in the spotlight of Dasiy's imploring gaze.

"Go swimming?" she asked, placing her warm hands on either side of Kessa's face.

"You don't know how to swim. We need to wait for the grown-ups and get you a floatie. Then you can start practicing."

"I a fishy!" She sucked her cheeks in and made a kissy face with her lips.

"No, you're a cutie!" she said, poking Daisy on the belly. "Would you like to be a character in my story? I could make you a fish or a mermaid or anything you want to be." Kessa kissed her apple cheek and looked into her stormy eyes, wild and sweet like a hot summer rain. She wondered what Daisy would be like as a teenager, but it was impossible to imagine. It was a character she couldn't write, even if she tried. Who are you, Daisy? she thought. Who will you be when you grow up? What kind of stories will you tell yourself when you lie awake at night?

Chapter 7: Worthless Matches

"And then, she went out to the back porch with—get this—a can of beer, to paint or whatever artsy stuff she does back there. She was going to leave Daisy playing by herself beside the sooty fireplace." Kessa had the old bulky landline phone wedged between her shoulder and her ear as she attempted to pour a glass of orange juice from the fridge while giving Toria a rundown of yesterday's events.

Toria let out an exasperated sigh. "Ugh! Little babies need naps and a schedule and nutritional food. They can't wander around all day eating cookies. It sounds like they don't just do unschooling—they must do unparenting too. Unreal! And what kind of mother starts drinking in the morning and then neglects their baby for the rest of the day?"

"Well, I guess she lets Daisy sleep on the couch whenever she gets tired, and they can all have as much junk food as they want whenever they feel like it. But it's always been that way for Arthur and Millie," Kessa added before taking a sip of her juice. "Maybe Daisy isn't used to the program yet. Also, I think technically she's not a baby. She's a toddler."

"That's no way to take care of a child," Toria said. "When I watch my little sister, I always make sure she has everything she needs, and I play with her too, and at nap time, my mom brings her a bottle and she goes in her crib. My mom says all kids need a routine."

Kessa had never seen Toria's baby sister, ten-month-old Audrina, with chips and cookies in her fists. Audrina always had lots of toys to play with too. Ones with bright colors and light-up buttons that said the alphabet. But maybe Daisy didn't actually care if she had proper baby toys, since she really seemed to like playing with sticks from the fireplace and scattering LEGO pieces and crunching chips with her feet.

"Daisy seems pretty happy," Kessa said, picking at the dirt beneath her nails. "Except when her mom doesn't want to pick her up. And Arthur and Millie turned out okay, so I guess it's probably fine. They just do things differently over there."

"How different do they have to do things before you are going to call Child Protective Services on them?" Toria said, a slippery iciness coating her voice.

Kessa sat down at the table in the dining room with her glass of juice. Its orangeness seemed too vivid to be real. "That seems extreme. The kids are a little messy, but they're not in danger or anything."

"Kess!" Toria shouted into the phone. "You said the child plays in the flippin' fireplace!"

"Not with a fire going!" Kessa shouted back. "Look, I don't want to start trouble. I'm just saying, if Daisy doesn't have someone to watch her, and Arthur and Millie don't want to do it, then why doesn't Candice ask me to babysit? I mean, I would love to earn some cash this summer."

"Yeah, it's weird how she just expects you to change diapers and stuff when you're over there. For free."

"It's like she would rather do her art than be around any of her kids. Though, honestly, Arthur and Millie really don't seem to care."

"They're probably used to having to fend for themselves. So anyway," Toria said, changing the subject, "I forget—what time exactly will you be turning thirteen tonight? I want to make sure I sing 'Happy Birthday' at that precise moment, wherever I am."

Kessa giggled. "Even if you're out in a store? You would just stop shopping, stand there, and start singing?" She smiled at the thought.

"Girl, you know I will!" Toria said and started to hum the tune.

"Well, you will probably be in bed," Kessa said, "because it's at 9:13. I asked my mom, and she dug out my birth certificate. She's sure it's the right time."

"In bed? Are you nuts?" Toria cried. "No, no, no. I will be watching Paranormal Perpetrators with my sisters. There's no way I'd miss it. They're going to a haunted mansion in New Orleans. I'll just have to sing for you at a commercial."

Paranormal Perpetrators was a reality TV show about ghost hunters who tried to solve crimes about bad things that happened to people in historical places. Toria loved stuff like that, and lucky for her, her two older sisters were always up late with the television on.

"Oh, you know, that reminds me," Toria said. "I want to look up your rising sign, now that I know the exact time. Hold on just a second."

Kessa had seen the signs before on one of Toria's books that her aunt Mercedes had given her. It was a thick and dog-eared paperback with a circle of symbols wrapped around the phases of the moon on the cover. The book had a specific sweet and smoky smell that was unlike anything else. Kessa could still remember the first time Toria had brought it out, proudly laying it on the puffy quilted top of her bed.

"There are answers in here," Toria had said with an unmistakable note of desperation, as if discovering a Gideons bible for the first time in a motel drawer. "Because of this book, I now know I can never date a Taurus, Cancer, or Virgo."

"But with twelve signs, that's got to be at least . . ." Kessa did the math in her head. ". . . a quarter of the whole population. Why limit yourself like that?"

"Why waste time on worthless matches?" Toria stroked the worn binding with her thumb. "You just don't get it."

The book that seemed to give Toria countless answers only left Kessa with more questions. The last time she had seen the book, it had been tucked away in a box beneath Toria's bed where she kept the other things her tía had given her, like crystals, incense, and jars of dried herbs. They were the kinds of things Mercedes sold in her shop where she worked as a psychic.

"Hold on, Kess, I'm just plugging in your dates and time. I found a website that calculates everything automatically."

"Do you still have that book with the matches?" Toria didn't answer, but Kessa could hear music in the background as she waited for the results. She rhythmically tapped the side of her foot against the chair leg and examined the polish on her fingers. It was already chipping, and she hadn't brought any nail polish with her. Not that she had anyone to impress, but she liked to think that her best match wouldn't care about things like that anyway.

In her daydreams, when she was an entirely different girl, her best match might be impressed that she had a best-selling novel or that she was too naturally pretty to cover her face with makeup. "You're beautiful just the way you are," he would say and she would read to him from the book she wrote, and the rhythm of her prose would cause him to touch her hand gently, like a butterfly landing on her wrist. He would lean in to kiss her, and she would let him, because he was vegan and because he loved her, just the way she was.

But none of that mattered at the moment. She didn't have to think about any of that, and her summer was free of worries about impending romance and other things. After all, she hadn't even shaved yet. There just never seemed to be a good time.

"Oh, interesting," Toria said, half whispering. "You're a Pisces rising. That makes so much sense. And you're a Cancer sun, and your moon sign is also Cancer. That is a lot of water in your chart. I mean, I'm not surprised. But Mars in Aries," she mumbled. "Wasn't expecting that."

"What does it all mean?" Kessa asked. "I have a lot of watery stuff?"

"Kessa, these descriptions go deep. I'll have to email it to you."

"But I probably won't get it unless I go into town. No internet, remember? Can't you just give me a preview?"

"I have to say, I think you might be a little bit psychic. Most people with this much water in their astro-chart are going to be very intuitive. My tía, she's got both Pisces and Cancer in her chart, loads of Scorpio too. It says here that you likely have a propensity for psychic dreams, a great imagination, and a deeply creative side."

"Sounds about right. My imagination is why I daydream so much, but that's also probably why I'm into writing. I don't know about the psychic part, but if I have any dreams about the future, I'll let you know!"

"You won't know if it was a dream about the future until that event has come to pass," Toria said pointedly. "Anyway, happy birthday, Kess. I'll be thinking about you tonight during Paranormal Perpetrators. Oh, I purchased a new lipstick today. Thanks to you, I was able to tell which ones were vegan. KVD Vegan Beauty is a good one and you can get all their stuff at Sephora."

Kessa frowned and looked into her empty glass. "Maybe I'll give lipstick a try this year," she said, though her thoughts were as far away from makeup as they could possibly be.

Could I really be psychic? Are my dreams able to predict the future? She put her juice glass in the sink and went to sit out on the back porch to watch the water. The clouds that darkened the sky made the lush green of the trees on the other side of the lake look especially vivid. She propped her feet up on the railing and leaned back in the chair, watching a cluster of dragonflies hover near the dock. Though she was, indeed, out in the middle of nowhere, it was probably one of the prettiest middle-of-nowheres one could possibly be.

Chapter 8: Life Goes On

"Wow! It looks so . . ." Kessa searched for a word to describe the cake on the table before her. "Yummy!" she said graciously. The birthday cake that Arthur and Millie had made was two round layers, one sliding off the other. There was a pile of sprinkles right in the center of the cake, and an oozy icing pooled all around the plate it sat on.

"Daisy did the sprinkles!" Millie said, beaming. "The sprinkle mountain was her idea. I bet this is going to taste amazing."

"Thanks, guys," Kessa said in her most cheerful tone. She didn't want them to know that she thought it was the ugliest cake she had ever seen. Usually her dad baked her birthday cake each year using boxed cake mixes from the store and applesauce in place of eggs, but this year, Arthur and Millie had wanted to try baking from scratch. Now Kessa found herself rather hesitant about sampling their handiwork.

"It's not about how it looks. The most important thing is how it tastes," Arthur said as though he had just read her thoughts.

"Oh, absolutely!" Kessa nodded.

"Wait. We need to light the candles." Her dad leaned over the table and dotted the cake with thirteen little pink-and-white sticks. Kessa wasn't sure the top layer would even stay on long enough for her to blow them all out. "And these are soy candles. Not beeswax."

"Thanks, Dad." Kessa smiled as the glow from thirteen candles cast a warmth beneath her chin.

"And the frosting is made from cashews," Millie said. "It's a totally vegan cake. It wasn't even that difficult, right, Arthur?"

"Yeah, I found a bunch of vegan recipe books at the library. We can try making something next time you're over." He gave her a lopsided smile and put his hands into his back pockets.

She was surprised by how good the cake actually tasted, and when everybody had eaten their piece, Millie thrust her present in Kessa's face and demanded it be opened first. Kessa peeled the handmade wrapping paper off a small white box with size 5 written on the side. She looked up at Millie, eyebrows raised.

"Those aren't baby shoes. That's just the box I used."

"Oh." Kessa laughed and pulled a wad of tissue paper from the small shoebox and unfurled it with care. Inside were tiny people no longer than her pinkie, with colorful dresses made of string. "These are beautiful! Thanks, Millie."

"They're worry dolls," Millie said proudly. "Give any worry you have to any of the dolls and then put it under your pillow. In the morning, your worry will be gone. I can say with one hundred percent confidence that it works at least fifty percent of the time."

Arthur put his gift down on the table and scratched at the back of his neck. "I don't know if you'll like this, but I can return it if you don't. It's no big deal."

She opened the small package and felt the weight of its contents drop into her hand. It was a compass with an engraving on it.

Go confidently in the direction of your dreams! Live the life you've imagined.

"A lot of people think that's a Thoreau quote, but that's a misconception. He didn't say it exactly like that. But I thought it sounded nice anyway."

"I love it," Kessa said. "I never learned how to use one, though. Maybe we could go try it out sometime, and you can show me what to do."

Arthur's cheeks reddened, and his lower lip twitched with the slightest hint of a smile. "All right, then."

Kessa's dad cleared his throat and placed his gift on the table before her, then leaned back in his chair and folded his arms. "This is something you've been wanting. I think it's about time too."

She tore off the newspaper wrapping and held up the box, grinning as she read it. "A portable hot spot!"

"It's an excellent wireless router for rural areas. That's what the reviews said, anyway. We can set it up tomorrow."

"So I can use the internet on my phone with this? And text too?" Kessa turned the box over and looked at the picture of the router on the back. She marveled at how such a small device could change everything for her. She would be able to stay in touch with Maddy and Toria by texting and go online anytime without asking her dad to drive her to the library or waiting to hit a serviced area on the way to the grocery store.

"And this is from your mom." He handed her a simple white envelope. Inside was a yellow piece of construction paper shaped like a bookmark and decorated with animal stickers from Kessa's craft drawer at home. It said: A $200.00 donation to Pennacook Pines Animal Sanctuary has been made in your honor. Kessa smoothed the strip of paper against the table. "Ruth is going to be so happy!"

"Indeed. She's already received the check from your mother and is looking forward to seeing you next week."

"I can't wait to go!"

"Great. Now, let's get this party started." He slid back his chair and made his way into the living room. Moments later, "Revolution" by the Beatles started booming from the giant old speakers on the floor, and Millie hopped up out of her chair and they all moved to the living room. When Kessa began jumping and twisting in the center of the carpet, Arthur startled her by grabbing her hand. Without warning, he twirled her around as if he'd been spinning unsuspecting partners all his life.

"I didn't know you could dance!" Kessa shouted over the music as Arthur sent her into another spin.

"Are you kidding?" Millie said. "He's amazing. We've been practicing for months, right, Arthur? We know the foxtrot too."

Arthur nodded. "Free dance lessons at the community center every other Wednesday night. You should come sometime."

Kessa felt her cheeks go hot as Arthur leaned in and pressed his hands against hers. "It's easy," he said. "Watch me. Just do this, okay? Step, step, rock step." Arthur let her hands go and grabbed Millie, who grinned from ear to ear as he demonstrated with her.

"He can flip me too. Arthur, do the flip," Millie begged as Arthur swooped and danced Millie across the floor. They whirled around the room a few times before Arthur scooped her up and flipped her over his shoulder in one fluid movement.

Breaking away from Millie, he faced Kessa once again, bringing his hands up firmly to lead her through another set. He looked at her steadily, not needing to glance down, while Kessa cast her own eyes downward to her clumsy bare feet. She stumbled at first but then found an awkward sort of rhythm. Arthur and Millie had made it look easy.

"There. You've got it!" Arthur smiled and backed away as Kessa repeated the rock step. "This isn't exactly ideal music for swing dancing, but you really can't go wrong with the Beatles, right?"

"Oh, oh! Can you play 'Ob-La-Di, Ob-La-Da'?" Millie screeched. She jumped up and down, her red hair bouncing as Kessa's dad bent over his record player.

"You got it, kiddo!"

Millie clapped her hands and then spun in circles with her arms out as Arthur took a seat on the couch, resting his hand on Bucky's back.

Kessa stopped dancing for a moment and leaned forward to scratch the mosquito bites that dotted her legs. When she straightened, she caught Arthur's gaze, but only briefly. He might not have been looking at her; maybe he had just been looking past her. It was hard to tell, because his eyes darted away so quickly, leaving her with her own anxious breaths feathering at the roof of her mouth.

She chewed on her pinkie nail, but it didn't matter. The polish was almost gone anyway. Kessa needed the music now more than ever. She needed the way it wrapped around her like a well-loved blanket. Something she knew the fabric of, intimately, its predictable pattern safe and familiar as it ever was.

Chapter 9: The Many Secrets of Six

Kessa sat out on the back porch as the sky finally grew dim over the lake. It hadn't been the worst birthday—not the best either, but at least the cake had been good. Unexpectedly good. She closed her eyes and breathed in the summer softness of the humid evening air. The breeze rushed through the trees and a front of gray-blue clouds, heavy with the possibility of rain, edged across the fading horizon.

In only an hour, she would be thirteen.

Most kids going into seventh grade wouldn't be turning thirteen until sometime during the school year, after classes had already gotten underway, after thousands of fallen leaves had been crunched underfoot and, later, when snow and ice glazed over the bare trees like tortured skeletons made of glass. Her mom had told her that she would always be one of the oldest in her grade because she had taken an extra year of preschool.

When Kessa had entered kindergarten, nervous and a bit taller than the rest, she had met Toria. There, in the cozy reading corner with the rainbow rug, they shared a giant bean bag and discovered that they were both sixes in a sea of fives—a sea of noisy, interrupting, nose-picking fives. The Special Six Club was what they called it. They made themselves a meeting place beneath the sprawling wooden structure in the play yard at recess and huddled in mulch-scented shadows, shoulder to shoulder, whispering the many secrets of six. It only lasted for a few months, though, because then Toria left the Special Six Club and became a Lucky Seven all on her own.

When Toria had turned thirteen last year, when the days fell back into darkness and the sun slipped away during their late afternoon snack, Toria hadn't made a big deal of it. But then, so many teenagery things had already happened to her at twelve. She'd held hands with a boy on the bus even though he had once thrown a ball at her face and damaged one of her front teeth. "It wasn't on purpose," Toria had said. But it had been. Everyone had seen it. They never did more than hold hands, but it still counted for something. Also, she received a secret driving lesson from her older sister Martina and had returned, swinging her long dark hair, claiming that driving was "a piece of cake." Most notably, she had started her period at eleven and had the first tell-tale bumps beneath her shirt to go with it.

The raindrops came spaced out, yards between each drop, and as Kessa stood up to head inside, a loud rustling on the side of the house caught her attention. She peered over the porch railing. A few small sticks and leaves sprinkled down, and a familiar furry tail poked through the leaves of the old maple tree.

This squirrel had been greeting her at the lake house regularly for years. Sometimes he would be so bold as to come right up to the back door, at any hour of the day, looking for handouts, but tonight he scrambled back and forth on his perch like her mom looking for misplaced keys in a hurry.

"Hold on, buddy!" Kessa said as she dashed inside and returned with a dilapidated leftover chunk of her ugly but delicious birthday cake. She set it down on the faded wooden deck floor and clicked her tongue a few times. "Dinner's ready. Sorry it's late." She didn't wait for him to come get it—she knew he would. He often took his treats like an artful thief, grabbing the loot only when her back was turned.

• • •

Kessa sank into the old mattress in her room on the second floor and took in the familiar surroundings. The wallpaper was peeling away in some places, but she loved its detailed antique flower motif. There was something timeless and quaint about it, like old-fashioned doll clothes. When she was little, before she fell asleep, she used to stare at all the different flowers and try to decide which one was the prettiest.

A refreshing chill seeped in through the open crack of the window, and each time the breeze billowed out the curtains, the rain would pelt faster, like horses picking up speed before fading to a gentle a trot.

She pulled the blue-and-white-patterned quilt up to her chin and let the ticking of rain against the window filter through a corner of her mind that she liked to visit at bedtime. It was a nighttime daydream she had first created when she was six, and she still used it to help her relax.

In this fantasy, she lay on a covered raft just big enough to shelter one queen-sized bed. And she drifted. She drifted down a stream lined with dense willows, their canopy so thick she couldn't even see the sky. Sometimes she let one hand hang out the small side opening to trail her fingers along in the easy current. The vaulted tent around her kept her dry from the galloping rain as she passed exotic banks covered in toadstools and giant curling ferns.

When the floating river bed failed to cruise her toward dreamland, Kessa glanced at the seashell-bordered clock hanging on the wall beside the door. She could barely make out the placement of its shadowed hands. 9:11? The digital clock on her dresser displayed the numbers 9:10 in glowing green.

Officially thirteen years old in two or three minutes.

Passing another year was nothing scary or unexpected. It was all the unknowns that loomed months and years ahead that kept her awake. The dreaded what-ifs.

What if she never met a boy worth kissing? What if Maddy and Toria were in all the same classes next year and she didn't know anybody in hers? What if she could never learn how to drive? What if she failed too many classes and couldn't pass on to high school, or worse, what if she failed high school and would never be allowed to go to college? What if the worry dolls tucked beneath the pillow didn't work and she woke the next morning with a racing heart and a stomach filled with the same churning, undigested thoughts?

The worry dolls were almost certain not to work, but it was worth a try. She had given each of them a name, whispering her darkest concerns at their awkward, stitched-on faces. It wasn't playing with dolls, no—it was something else. It was like a spell. But where was the magic?

Now, it was the flowers on the wallpaper that caught her attention. She squinted a bit and tried to focus. Were her eyes playing tricks on her? No, she could definitely see movement. The flowers began to turn, slowly at first but then picking up the pace like hundreds of spinning toy tops, and a whirring sound filled the room. The smaller painted-on buds were blooming like new butterflies opening their wings to the night. A buzzing sensation ran through her arms and legs, vibrations that came in waves and made her skin prickle all over.

She pressed her eyes closed for a moment and gripped the bedsheets, but when she opened her lids again, the flowers were still moving, and now the vines seemed to be coming straight out of the wall. She opened her mouth, but all she could do was inhale, sucking the perfumed air into her lungs like a vacuum on high. Her body was glued to the mattress, all of her muscles frozen in place.

The flowers spun in their dizzy circles, filling the room with the fragrance of a summer bouquet. The sweet rose mingled with the unmistakable scent of lilacs and lavender, casting a sleepy and disoriented haze around the room. A cloudy fog pushed through her lips and dissolved into a pleasant sweetness, light as cotton candy on her tongue.

Blossoms of tannin red and blushing coral rushed around the room on invisible currents and multiplied. A single pale-pink petal floated down and landed right on her nose like an outstretched tongue awaiting a snowflake. When she exhaled, the warm puff of air sent a flurry of color swirling about her head like an enchanted blizzard. A forceful breeze rushed through the window, and when the curtains billowed out, thousands of more petals came whooshing in.

Somehow, through the pastel storm of petals, she made out the form of a small woodchuck hovering in midair and blinking its eyes, an aura of flowers clinging to its furry coat. It wasn't Chuck Chuck, of course; Chuck Chuck was back at home and just a raggedy stuffed animal. This woodchuck was real and smiling at her with a broad Cheshire-cat grin. Can woodchucks smile? It didn't matter—she wanted to slip away into this new and flowery world like Alice into her Wonderland. Whatever was happening to her, it held far more enchantments than her old drifting-river-bed dreamscape.

She closed her eyes and breathed in as another gust of air sailed through the window and caressed the stray wisps of hair around her face. She thought of her late grandmother, how she would lightly drag her nails across Kessa's scalp before weaving a bedtime braid that kept the strands in place for the night. There was just no other way to describe it: it was an exquisite sensation.

Part Two

Chapter 10: It Is True

"Kessa? Are you ready to get up, sleepyhead? I made vegan pancakes."

Kessa opened her eyes to see her dad standing in the doorway. A shaft of bright morning light poured in through the part in the curtains. Her dad never made pancakes, let alone vegan ones. Did he even have baking powder or know how to use vinegar in the almond milk to get them extra fluffy?

"What time is it?"

"It's nine a.m. already. I thought you might like to come to the store with me today. We could go to the big grocery store and get some nice treats. I'm running out of snacks, and that vegan cream cheese you like is almost gone." He smiled his funny crooked smile, walked over to the edge of her bed, and plopped down. White patches of flour dotted his old baggy blue jeans. "Maybe we could get some more vegan cookies? I might have eaten just a few of those . . ." He scratched his head and gave her a sheepish look.

"Dad!" she said, sitting up with a giggle. "You ate almost the entire package."

"And I'm going to buy us a new package." He patted the

lump on the blanket where she had gathered her legs up under the covers. "Two new packages, as a matter of fact. One for each of us. Sound good?"

"Okay, I'll get dressed and be down in a few mi—" Her heart skipped a beat as she looked past her dad to the flower-print wallpaper, memories of last night flooding her mind. She squinted at it, but it was normal and still. Just ordinary, unanimated wallpaper.

"What's the matter? You okay? There's no rush. Just come down when you're ready." Her dad stood up and brushed the flour off his jeans. "It's a little cool out this morning. The rain last night brought in a chill, so you might want to wear a sweater for now until it warms up. See ya downstairs—don't let the pancakes get cold." He gave the doorway a tap with his hand on the way out.

Kessa sprang out of bed as soon as she heard him walking down the stairs. She ran over to the wallpaper and ran her fingers along the vines between each cluster of flowers, like tracing paths on a map.

"It wasn't a dream. I know it wasn't," she whispered with her nose pressed up against a pink rose. She drew the covers up to make the bed in a haphazard fashion, fluffed the big pillow, and threw it down. It landed with a poof against the headboard.

Kessa watched, wide-eyed, as a single pink petal whooshed up into the air before floating down softly onto the middle of the quilted bedspread.

• • •

On the way to the store, Kessa sat in the front seat beside her dad with one hand in the pocket of her favorite oversized gray hoodie. She squeezed the pink petal between her thumb and forefinger as if she could somehow press the magic from it. That one silky little petal was the only remaining evidence that something extraordinary and unexplainable had happened last night. Had it all been a hallucination? A dream? Or had the rainstorm somehow loosened thousands of petals from nearby blossoms? And what about the smiling woodchuck—what was that all about?

There was nothing but dense forest on either side of the road, and the trees rushed past in a blur of green. "Dad? Do we have any roses on the property?"

"I don't think so. I've never planted any." He raised an eyebrow at her. "Did you want to? Or grow herbs maybe? We do have that little garden on the side of the house. It needs some work and hasn't been used in years, but I can help you weed it out if you'd like to do some gardening this year. Maybe you and Arthur and Millie can make a project out of it. We can stop at Moosehead General Garden and pick out some nice seedlings on the way home."

"I think I would like to plant stuff, but not flowers. Things we can eat and use in recipes." Kessa reached for her phone to see if it was getting any reception. "Is my phone going to work at the store? I'm probably missing a million Toria selfies right now." Kessa rolled her eyes as she powered on her cell.

Her dad chuckled. "Toria the beauty queen? How has she been?"

"She said she's only going to be buying cruelty-free makeup from now on, now that she knows how to look for the right labels. I'm glad, but I just feel like if someone is really concerned about cruelty to animals, then maybe they shouldn't . . ." Kessa cleared her throat and looked at her dad out of the corner of her eye. ". . .you know, eat them?"

He glanced at her quickly before setting his eyes back on the road. "You know, I've been thinking. I'm going to be vegan—well, uh, I mean plant-based—while you're here. Since I have to cook vegan meals anyway, it makes sense not to make two different things. And not to brag, but my pancakes this morning did come out pretty good."

"Oh, Dad! Are you serious? That's awesome!"

"Absolutely. Will you help me find everything we need at the store?"

"Of course! Let's have vegan lasagna tonight. I can even make a cashew cheese for it. And once we've started our garden, we'll have tons of herbs to use. And we need to get some turmeric and onion powder so I can show you how to make tofu scramble the good way. Seriously, Dad, once you see how easy and yummy it is, you won't feel the need to eat animals anymore, even after I've gone back home to Mom. I mean, Bucky is an animal, and you would never eat him, so why eat any of the others? They deserve to live just as much as Bucky, right?"

"Oh, well, yes, that may be true." He smiled and gave her a pat on the leg.

It is true, Kessa thought, and she wanted to say it, but those three little words seemed to flatten against the roof of her mouth, her tongue pressing them like a piece of gum waiting to be bubbled out between her lips.

"You know, I'm really proud of you, Kessa. You always stick up for what you think is right."

What I know is right, she thought, fixing her eyes on the smattering of puffy white forms in the sky. But she wasn't one to be stubborn; it didn't agree with the clouds. Unlike Toria, the pacing of the universe always seemed to eclipse her. Words in edgewise were never worth the effort anyway, so she filed them away in the far corners of her mind, for other times and other stories, places that were just as slow and wandering and flowery as she liked it, purple as a rambling page of prose.

Chapter 11: It's Hard to Explain

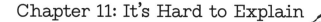

Kessa unloaded several trays of seedlings from the trunk and back seat as her dad brought in the groceries. The tomato plants looked even bigger now than they had at the checkout. Even the herbs seemed taller. She leaned over a tuft of chives and inhaled the pleasant scent. She sniffed the mint, basil, and dill too. The dill was pretty, with a lacey-looking softness, and she couldn't help but pass her fingertips over its delicate fronds. Without any warning, the plant shivered up about an inch between her fingers.

"Dad? I think . . . I think our plants are already growing," she said, eyeing the dill carefully for any more signs of movement.

He walked in and placed a bag on the counter. "Oh really?" he said as he began taking things out and setting them in the fridge.

"Yeah. I just saw this one grow." Kessa pointed to the dill plant. "I literally saw it."

"Well, you don't exactly see plant growth in action. It happens gradually."

"But I touched the plant and it wiggled upward about an inch. It really did!"

"Well, maybe you just have a green thumb." Her dad winked at her and stuck a gallon of almond milk in the fridge and shut the door. "Let me know when you're ready to start prepping for dinner and I'll come down and help. I have a few more hours of writing to do." He headed toward the stairs, then added, "Oh, will you let Bucky out, please? He's been having a lot more accidents lately."

"Sure," Kessa said. She gave the plants on the table a warning look and went to go find Bucky. "Where's my favorite little bagel beagle?" she called into the living room. He wasn't in his usual spot on the couch. She picked up his chew toy and went out to the front hallway, but what she heard stopped her in her tracks.

"I'm in here." A distant and weak voice responded. It was coming from the side room where the writing nook was. Had somebody snuck into the house while they were out? She took another step down the hallway, listening intently, but could only hear the distinct clinking sound of Bucky's collar.

Kessa stood with her back to the wall and then carefully peeked into the room. Nobody was in there except Bucky, who approached her with a limp tail wag.

"Hey there, you wanna go out?" Kessa gave a little whistle and squeezed his chew toy.

"Oh, you brought my favorite toy. I can hardly see it, but I can tell by the smell. Thank you, dear." Bucky ambled passed Kessa, down the steps, and out to the front lawn, where he sniffed at the patchy grass.

Did Bucky just speak to her? She watched from the steps as he walked around in a few circles and then crouched beside the large bush on the side of the porch.

"Some privacy would be nice," the voice said weakly as Bucky looked right at her with his chin held high.

She put her hands over her ears and looked away. This can't be happening. Dogs don't talk! Kessa sat down on the porch steps, stunned into silence as Bucky approached her.

"I'm so old now that maybe I should just wear a diaper." He chuckled and cocked his head, questioning Kessa with his watery eyes.

"How can you be talking? Your mouth isn't even moving!" She offered him the chew toy she was still holding, which Bucky tugged at playfully for a few minutes. When she finally let him have it, he opened his mouth and let the raggedy toy drop to the ground.

"I'm afraid I'm too tired for games. As it is, I'm due for my midday nap. You'll let me in won't you, dear?" He limped up the porch stairs and put his nose against the screen.

Kessa hopped to her feet and opened the door. Bucky ambled in and made his way to the living room to find his favorite spot on the couch.

"Are you really talking to me in my mind, or have I gone completely nuts?" Kessa said. Bucky just curled up on the couch and closed his eyes.

She stroked his fur. Was something wrong with her? She didn't feel unwell, but with the dill plant growing from her lightest touch and now her dog talking, well, it was enough to make her question her sanity, especially after the wallpaper flowers last night. She was beginning to feel quite dizzy and could almost hear her mom chiding her for not eating soon enough. Blood sugar. She dragged herself into the kitchen.

When she sat down at the table to eat her sandwich, she could have sworn that the plants bent, ever so slightly, in her direction. With trembling fingers, she put her hand out and held it over the small basil plant. Its leaves wavered beneath her palm, and something in her peripheral vision moved, shifting her attention to a scuttling sound that rippled across the wooden slats of the back porch. She opened the screen door and caught her dusty-gray squirrel climbing out onto a far-reaching limb of the old maple tree, where he stopped to munch on something.

"Are you spying on me?" Kessa said, putting her hands on her hips. She leaned over the railing, trying to get a closer look, but the cordless phone, ringing in its cradle, called her back inside.

"Hey, Kess. I'm sorry I didn't call yesterday," Maddy said on the other end of the line. "I had a swim meet and by the time it was over, my mom said it was too late to be on the phone."

"That's okay. I know how busy you are in the summer."

"How was your birthday? Did you get anything good?"

"Well, my dad got me a portable Wi-Fi hot spot so I can get online. We're going to set it up later today. Millie gave me worry dolls, and Arthur gave me a compass, a really fancy one. My mom sent a donation for the sanctuary out here."

"That's awesome! I have a present for you here. It's a vegan recipe book. You can get it when you come back!"

"Thanks, Madds, you're the best," Kessa said, ducking back out to the porch and scanning the tree.

"So what else is new?"

"It's hard to explain." She paused, replaying the recent events in her head. The strangeness of it all. What could she possibly say that wouldn't make it seem like she had lost her mind? "Maddy?" she ventured. "Have you ever had something unexplainable happen to you before?"

"What do you mean, like ghosts or spirits?"

"Yeah, something like that." The squirrel was now perched on the limb, stock-still, not a whisker out of place. He was definitely watching her.

The little spy.

"Well, this one time, after my grandma died, I went into the kitchen, and it smelled like her perfume. It was a really strong smell, and it's not a common perfume. Anyway, my gram liked to cook, so I thought it was interesting that I was smelling it in the kitchen. I guess I like to think it was really her, that maybe she was giving me a sign or something." Maddy grew quiet for a moment. "I know it sounds impossible, but I know what I smelled. I know it."

"Wow. That's really special." Kessa cleared her throat, pressing on with her next question. "Have you ever had thoughts come into your mind that seemed like they weren't yours?"

"I believe that's a mental condition called schizophrenia." Maddy laughed. "You aren't hearing things, are you, Kess? If you are, that's very serious, and you need to tell someone."

"I'm not hearing things that aren't real. I mean, no, I'm not having a mental breakdown. I was just thinking about psychics. How do they know things? A psychic might be able to hear someone's thoughts, right?"

"Have you been talking to Toria lately? Is she doing her astrology stuff on you?" Maddy asked with suspicion.

"She did do an astrological chart, but that's not important. I was just wondering how psychics do telepathy, mind reading, that kind of thing."

"They don't. It's all show, a scam to get your money. Think about it: If spirits could make contact or send signs like my gram did for me, wouldn't they just go right to the person they wanted to talk to? Why would they make a connection through another person who doesn't even know them? Anybody can call themselves a psychic, Kess, literally anyone. Even the famous ones with their own shows are phonies. It's all set up ahead of time. Even Toria's aunt is kind of a scam artist because she charges money for all that garbage."

"How do you know it's all fake?"

Maddy scoffed. "Kessa! It's nonsense. Everybody knows."

Nonsense. It wasn't exactly the answer she was hoping for. After the call, Kessa placed the phone on the glass table next to the porch chair. She spotted the squirrel again, but now he was down by the base of the tree digging around in the dirt. She tore off the crusts from her sandwich and ripped them into small bits before chucking them over the railing.

"Hey, li'l guy. Do you have anything to say to me? Anything?" she said. He dashed out to retrieve the bread and, like a furry bolt of lightning, scooted right back under the shade of the maple. "Wait, I need to ask you something," she called, but he scurried away into the brush beyond the gnarled roots of the tree, quick and nameless as the current behind the clouds.

Chapter 12: Writing and Weeding

"It's a good start." Kessa's dad rose from the seat in the writing nook, nodding his head, but the corners of his mouth turned down, as if he were approving an adequate meal.

Adequate but not spectacular.

"But?" She knew he was holding back. She wanted a real critique, she told herself. She could handle it.

"Well." He tapped his lower lip and squinted at the document on the computer screen. "Your main character doesn't have any agency."

"Agency?"

"Your character has to make choices and push the story along. This girl in your story, for example—so far, things are just happening to her. She's merely a passenger. Strong, dynamic characters will take the wheel every now and then. Does she make any of her own decisions? How will her choices affect the story? It could be the difference between a mediocre piece of work and something your readers will want to invest in."

"So you're saying my story is boring?" She wanted feedback, but she didn't think it would hurt so much. It was almost as if he was calling her boring. But maybe it was dull; maybe it really wasn't good. Maybe none of her work had ever been as great as she had thought it was.

Perhaps, all this time, she had been asking the wrong people for their opinion. Her teachers usually wrote comments on her creative writing assignments like "Great imagination" or "Wonderful use of metaphor and simile," but they weren't writers. This was different. This was the honest critique she had thought she wanted, and it smacked her in the face, heating her cheeks with all the tenderness of a fresh bee sting.

"Look, do you want to read about a princess who's been captured by a dragon and is waiting for a knight to come save her and marry her into 'happily ever after,' or would you rather read about a princess who slays the dragon herself, duels with the queen, and runs away to build her own kingdom?"

"The second one sounds more interesting."

"Right. Just something to keep in mind. But I do think there's a lot of potential here," he said, tapping the edge of the monitor. "Fleshing out characters and their arcs is a messy business, but it's worth it."

"What if my character is just an average girl, though? What if that's who she is and everything else about the story just happens to be more interesting than her?"

"Then maybe this average girl doesn't deserve to be the main character." He went over to the center bookshelf, the one with the sagging middle, and pulled a few novels off the top ledge. "These all have good examples of strong protagonists. You can't be a writer if you're not a reader." He placed them on the desk beside the computer and left the room humming.

She sat back down in the nook and focused on the screen, its punishing brightness a painful contrast to the dull content it displayed. Mediocre. Boring. Average. It made her eyes sting, but it wasn't too late. She had agency, after all.

• • •

"I just don't think vegetables and herbs are a good choice," Arthur said as he knelt before the garden bed full of weeds and overgrown grass. They hovered over it together, there on the side of the house as the late morning sun warmed their backs. "If you plant those things in here, they're going to get eaten by animals immediately, especially the parsley and the mint."

Kessa frowned and continued pulling the weeds out while wearing the pair of winter gloves she had found in the back of the coat closet. They seemed to be working to block whatever magic altered the plants from her barehanded touch, though they were rather hot and uncomfortable.

"I mean, I already got all this stuff. We have to plant it now. And besides, there must be some way to keep hungry critters out." She braced herself in a squatting position and struggled with a particularly well-rooted stalk with a thick stem.

"Hey, uh, what's with the gloves?" Arthur asked as he grabbed a few weeds and tossed them over his shoulder.

"I don't have proper garden gloves. And these are protecting my hands."

More like protecting the plants from me.

"Hi, guys!" Millie came up to them and offered her water bottle to Kessa before sitting down, right in a pile of pulled-up weeds.

"Well, are you going to help or not?" Arthur tossed a weed at her, and a clump of dirt landed in her fluffy curls.

"I helped!" she shouted, shaking out her hair. "By bringing the water."

"Thanks, Millie," Kessa said after swallowing a gulp. "If you want to do anything else, you can help with the rest of the weeds, and then I'm going to rake the soil a bit."

Arthur picked up the hand trowel and dug away at the dirt. "I don't know how you would have done all this without our help and my mom's garden tools. This is kind of a big job. Is your dad going to pitch in?"

"I don't know. He might later, but he's writing at the moment. I just really wanted to get started. The seedlings have been on the porch for a couple of days now."

Arthur stood up and began working the dirt with the rusty tiller he had brought over from their shed. "It's too late to do a raised bed. Maybe we can build a small fence around it."

Kessa raked the dirt with her gloved fingers and thought about how nice it would be to harvest her tomatoes when they ripened and to add little sprinkles of fresh herbs to her meals. How hard could it be to grow a few plants?

"I'm hungry," Millie moaned.

"You're always hungry," Arthur said as he looked at his watch. "It's only eleven!"

"Already?" Kessa stood up abruptly and pulled off her gloves. She smoothed a few stray hairs back with her sweaty palms. "I have to go let Bucky out now, but I'll be right back." She hurried over to the front of the house, where Bucky was already waiting, nose pressed to the screen door.

"Come on out." Kessa opened the door, and Bucky hobbled down the steps. He made a few circles and then went over to his usual spot by the large rhododendron bush. She turned her head away, remembering his privacy request from the last time.

"Thank you, dear, I'm already done." Bucky began walking back to her with his tongue hanging out, but he swayed and limped, making the short distance seem like a rather arduous trek.

"So, I guess I can still hear you," Kessa said as she sat down on the steps. "Lots of people talk to their dogs. It's not weird that I'm talking to you—it's only weird that I can actually hear what you're saying back. Right?" Kessa rubbed beneath his graying ears and put her head against his. "It will be our little secret, okay?"

"Will you let me inside, dear? My hips are aching, and I could really go for a biscuit right now." Bucky wagged his tail as he carefully made his way up the steps.

Kessa opened the door and followed him into the kitchen, where she took out the big plastic container of doggy biscuits and handed him one. She stooped over and rubbed his back as he devoured the treat. "When did you learn to communicate like this?"

Bucky looked at her as he crunched on his biscuit. "What do you mean? I've always communicated with you. Maybe you just weren't listening as well as you are now."

Kessa straightened, placing her hands on her hips. "I didn't know we could talk like this!" she exclaimed. "Nobody would believe me if I told them. Talking animals? It's totally bizarre."

"Humans are animals too. Every one of us has the ability to send our thoughts directly to another's mind. It's just that most people aren't aware that they can. They don't know how to use that part of their brain. You see? You can talk to me without using your voice just like other animals do." Bucky turned around and headed back to the living room.

Kessa didn't take her eyes off him as he used the small stool to get up onto his spot on the couch. *I'm going back out to work on the garden with Arthur and Millie. Let me know if you need to go out again.*

"That's it, my dear!" Bucky curled up on his blanket and smiled at her as only a dog can, tongue hanging loosely from the side of his grin. "Is there any way you can teach your father? I do so want to let him know how much I hate the new crunchy stuff he's been putting in my bowl lately."

"I'll tell him," she said aloud. She stood in silence for a moment as Bucky nuzzled the cushion and closed his eyes.

Sweet dreams, Bucky. I love you.

Chapter 13: Mihku

Kessa made her way down the steep steps of the back porch while holding the first tray of herbs to be planted. The last few days had been all rain, and now they were almost too big for their pots. She took a quick snap of the garden to send to Toria and Maddy so they could see the "before" picture and then set her cell phone down on the grass. It was nice being able to text again, and the Wi-Fi from the portable hot spot reached out into the yard well enough to get a signal, but she didn't want it to distract her from getting the garden ready.

Picking up the trowel Arthur had left out for her, Kessa stabbed at the earth and dug a series of holes for the plants. As she formed a second row, she spotted the mischievous squirrel watching her from the other side of the garden bed.

"There you are. Come to spy on me again, huh?" It seemed reckless to encourage this delusion, but if other animals could speak to her the way Bucky did, she wanted to know.

He stood very still with his head cocked to one side, staring and waiting.

Yes, he was ready.

And so was she.

Kessa gathered her thoughts like a bundle of wishing flowers and sent them his way, but those seeds of hope just fell silently between them. There was no squirrel voice floating into her mind. But of course there wouldn't be. She had known Bucky all her life; naturally he would be more comfortable talking to her than a wild squirrel who only visited the porch for handouts.

"Speaking of handouts, I've been meaning to thank you for the birthday cake."

"Ha! I knew it! So you can communicate," Kessa said, a smug smile tugging at the corners of her mouth.

The squirrel gave her a strange look and made little scrunchy movements with his nose. "Of course I can." He chuckled. "I can also tell you that cake was the best treat I've had in a long time. The cashew frosting was brilliant. I even brought some back for my friend Azeban—he's a raccoon, so you probably haven't met him. Night creatures, you know—such a sneaky bunch, always creeping around in the dark like they own the moon." He threw his tiny paws in the air and briefly raised his nose to the sky, then began sniffing the ground again. "So, do you have any more of that good bread crust from the other day?"

"I have lots of food I can give you." Kessa set her soil knife down and leaned forward on her elbows to have a closer look at her chatty friend. "But first I want to know more about you. What's your name? Do squirrels even have names? I'm Kessa, by the way. Kessa Caliper."

"Of course I have a name! Doesn't everybody? You can call me Mihku. Mihku Maskosit." Mihku scraped at the ground with his little paws and eyed Kessa carefully. "You don't even know why I'm here, do you?"

"Huh? What do you mean?" Kessa, with her face close to the dirt, spied some small weeds that she had missed, poking up through the ground like tiny sore thumbs.

Mihku puffed out his chest. "I am your animal helper. I'm supposed to help you understand your new skills and teach ya stuff. And apparently you have no idea how to plant a simple herb garden, so I guess we'll start there. These holes are too close together, for starters." The squirrel took a few hops and crouched next to the first hole Kessa had dug. "The plants need room for their root systems to develop. Space out your plantings."

"Wait, hold up. Animal helper? Teach me stuff?" Kessa eased herself back into a kneeling position. "Like what? Do you know about why I can suddenly hear animals talk and make plants grow by touching them? Or about the wallpaper flowers?"

"Wallpaper what now? Oh, that was Nokomis bringing your gift. Sometimes the whole thing gets a little flowery. Lemme guess." Mihku pointed his tiny paw at her. "You don't hurt animals, and it's probably been that way for about thirteen years, am I right?"

"Yes. I'm thirteen and I've never hurt an animal my whole life. I don't eat them either, of course. But what does that have to do with—"

"Your gift? Ah, well, when a human goes approximately thirteen whole years doing the least harm possible to all living things, this can happen—that is, if your mind is ready for it. Most people today are not ready at all. Nokomis doesn't just bestow her gifts upon anyone."

"You mean, there are others who have these abilities?"

"Some." Mihku paused. "But they are few and far between. Your mind has to be ready for it, and not many people have open minds, so people with this gift are rare." Mihku scrabbled in the dirt some more. "You really need to clear out these weeds!"

Without thinking, Kessa quickly plucked out a few of the small budding weeds with her bare hands and tossed them to the side. Surprisingly, they didn't move or wiggle or grow at all when she touched them, even though she hadn't yet put on her gloves. But she didn't have time to contemplate that—there was an actual, real, live squirrel talking to her, and nothing in the world could distract her from this moment. "Who is Nokomis?"

"Who is Nokomis?" Mihku chuckled. "Why, you really have a lot to learn, don't you? Nokomis is the reason for all of this"—he looked up toward the sun and raised his tiny arms to the sky—"for you and me, and for all living things."

"Oh, I see. So she's like Mother Earth or something like that?" Kessa cast her eyes out over the lake. The placid water grew dark for a moment as a cloud passed across the sun. "Is she some kind of goddess?"

"Think of her as your wise and kindly old grandmother—or a woodchuck!" Mihku laughed in a quick and squirrely way.

"A woodchuck?"

"Yes, she usually takes that form. We animals around the lake call her Grandmother Woodchuck." Mihku hopped even closer and put his little paw right on her knee. "Kessa?" he asked. "I like the sound of your name. What does it mean?"

"It doesn't have a meaning, but my middle name is Margalit. It means 'pearl.' Isn't that pretty? Does your name have a meaning?"

"All names have a meaning!" Mihku said sharply.

"So 'Mihku Maskosit' means what, then? Is that like your first and last name?"

"I don't want to tell you! It's—it's embarrassing." Mihku pulled his paw back and had just turned away from her when a buzzing came up through the earth, vibrating the grass. Mihku jumped, his whiskers twitching in alarm.

"Don't worry. It's just my cell." Kessa reached for her phone and flipped it over to see the screen. Toria had responded to her garden picture with a series of little green hearts and flower emojis. Kessa had only glanced down for a second, but when she looked up again, Mihku was gone. She scanned the slope toward the lake and across the lawn toward the wooded area that divided her property with Arthur and Millie's, but there was no sign of the squirrel.

"Mihku?" Kessa ran down the sloping green toward the back-porch steps. She eyed the sun-warmed dock resting calmly on the lake and then heard a familiar rustling coming from high up in the maple tree. It took her only a few moments to reach the top of the stairs and rush across the deck. Leaning over the railing, she looked up into the twisted maple, but all she saw was a small ordinary sparrow grooming its wings. "Mihku! Come back, please!"

"Kessa? Is that you? Are you okay?"

She craned her neck to see up the side of the house. Her dad poked his head out of his writing room window, working his eyes across the lake.

"I'm okay! I'm down here—on the porch!" She waved.

"Oh, all right, I just heard you yelling and wanted to make sure nothing was wrong. How's the planting going?"

She plopped into the metal folding chair and frowned at the other tray of seedlings she had yet to bring out, along with the two pots of tomato plants, which seemed to be getting taller every minute. "It's fine. I just have to make the holes farther apart," she yelled back. She heard the window screen slam down, and Kessa grabbed the remaining tray of seedlings and made her way back out to the garden.

Mihku was going to have to come back—he would have to. She still had so many questions. She would lure him back with more treats, offerings that a squirrel couldn't refuse. Maybe her dad wouldn't even notice if the new bag of his favorite trail mix went missing. Sometimes you just had to make things happen.

Chapter 14: Sippy

"I'm heading out to the pet store. Do you want to come along?" Kessa's dad peered into the small room off the front hallway where Kessa was snuggled next to Bucky on a giant bean bag.

"No thanks. I'm going to check on the garden soon, and Arthur said he would come over to help me with it." She gave Bucky a tacit nod and then addressed her dad. "Do you think you could get a different kind of food for Bucky? He doesn't like the current stuff. He hardly eats it."

"Well, Bucky has bad gums and his kidneys are not doing well—not to mention his eyes—so the vet says he needs a special diet."

"But look." Kessa ran her hand on the underside of Bucky's belly. "He's losing so much weight. That can't be good for him either."

"I don't know, Kess. I'll ask the vet. In the meantime, we need to stick with what I've been giving him." Bucky whimpered softly and turned his head to look at Kessa.

She shrugged. "I'm sorry, Bucky," she whispered into his floppy ear.

Her dad laughed. "You two and your secret language." He shook his head and grabbed the keys off the hook next to the front door. "I'll be back in a bit. Don't go down to the lake until I get back, okay?"

Kessa nodded and smoothed down Bucky's ears. She looked into his eyes. "I tried. Do you want a biscuit?"

Bucky rolled over and ambled into the hallway. "Yes, my dear, I would love a biscuit, and I don't give a whit about my kidneys either!" He stopped in front of the kitchen as Kessa grabbed the biscuits from above the fridge.

"Dad just wants you to stay healthy and live as long as possible. We both do." Kessa handed Bucky the treat and shook her head as he munched it up. "You need to try and eat your healthy food."

Bucky looked up at her with his bloodshot eyes, the foggy irises like pools of melted chocolate. "I've already lived a long time," he said weakly, lowering his head. "I'm not afraid to move on. I've been promised I'll be a coyote next time. I'll be fast and strong again with sharp eyes that can see through the night. That's what the old woodchuck said. I think the life of a coyote would suit me just fine."

"Don't say that." She didn't like hearing Bucky talk about "moving on," whether he got a new life as a coyote or not. He belonged by her side, by the lake, a permanent fixture of every childhood summer she had ever known. "I'm sure it would be nice to be a coyote, but right now, you have plenty of time to just be you. I'm going out to the garden. I'll come back in soon to let you out in case you need to go pee, okay?"

But Bucky was already asleep. Was he dreaming of coyote life? Kessa had an overwhelming urge to sit beside him and rest her head against his back, but she pushed herself out the door. The garden was waiting.

After stopping to fill the watering can with the hose beside the house, she approached the garden, eyes darting around for any signs of Mihku, but it was the raggedy bunch of stems poking through the soil that brought her to her knees.

"Oh no! The parsley."

The green shoots had been chewed down to stubs. Without a second thought, she ran her ungloved fingers across the broken stems. Tiny green curls began to sprout from the sides of the remaining shoots, and before she even had a chance to pull her hand away, a few of them wriggled upward. Even more small leaves began to unfurl from their tops. *My gloves!* She picked up the large winter mitts from the ground, shook the dirt out, and stuffed her sweaty hands inside as a singsongy voice floated through her mind.

"What are you doing that for? Don't you want the plant to grow?"

A little brown bird zoomed past her face and landed on the lawn about a yard away from where Kessa sat. She recognized it as the sparrow she had seen in the maple tree yesterday. The bird took a few light hops toward her and cocked its head to the side.

Even though Kessa should have been, by all recent accounts, used to animals talking to her, she was still taken off guard by this small bird, so clearly and freely communicating its thoughts to her.

"You can talk too?"

"Of course. I can also sing, dance, and act. I believe they call that a triple threat." She opened her brown wings, showing off the smooth white feathers beneath, and puffed out her tiny chest, which was speckled like cookies and cream. "So, you're the girl, the one with the Gift. When I saw that parsley quiver and grow from one little touch . . . well, I just knew it was true. I've never met a human child with the Gift. Quite remarkable!"

The sparrow ruffled its feathers and hopped like popped corn over toward the garden. It stopped right before the parsley, which now looked as full and lush as it had the day before.

"Your gift could really come in handy since it seems many creatures enjoy their parsley around here. Why don't you give it another touch? And maybe pass your hand over this dill while you're at it—it's looking a little scraggly," said the bird.

"Hey, hey! Sippy, back off. I'm her animal guide, not you!" Out of nowhere, Mihku came zipping across the lawn. He tried to stop but stumbled and landed right on top of a patch of mint. Mihku shook the soil off his furry back, sat up on his haunches, and looked right at Sippy, who was preening her wings beside the parsley.

The bird blinked and took a few hops toward Mihku. "I'm sorry to be the one to break this to you, Mihku, but Nokomis has assigned me to Kessa as well. She thought you could use some help."

Mihku lowered his head, and his whiskers quivered slightly. "She didn't think I could do it?"

"Oh, stop it." Sippy ruffled her feathers. "She just thought you could use some help is all. Anyway, I was asking the girl why she wanted to put on those dreadful gloves. It's like she doesn't even want to use the Gift. And it would be oh so useful right now, after the destruction that's come to this sweet little garden." Sippy flapped her wings as only an exasperated sparrow could; then she and Mihku fixed their shiny coal eyes on Kessa.

Her palms were growing increasingly damp and itchy, but the gloves were the suffocating protection she counted on. She pulled one off and held it up in the air like something she'd fished out of the garbage. "I have to wear these when I'm in the garden or else things could get out of control. I can't just be making every plant I touch grow all over the place. What if somebody were to see me?"

Sippy alighted upon Kessa's knee. She was so light that Kessa could barely feel the weight of her. "Oh no, it's not like that at all. You don't have to wear gloves all the time—why, that's just ridiculous." She gave Mihku a shrewd look. "Hasn't Mihku explained all this?"

"Hey! It's a lot to cover, okay?" Mihku scrabbled over to them, sat down, and sniffed at his feet. His nose wrinkled and he shook his head. "Darn! I thought landing in all that mint would at least help cover up the smell a little bit."

A light, lilting laugh arose from Sippy's throat like leaves fluttering up into the wind. "They don't call you Mihku Maskosit for nothing, do they?"

Mihku shot her a look. "Shut it, Sippy!"

Sippy looked up at Kessa with steady, unblinking eyes. "I'm sorry—I never formally introduced myself. My name is Sips Sahsapu, but most people call me Sippy."

Kessa held her bare hand out for Sippy, and she hopped right on. "My name is Kessa. You both have such interesting names. What do they mean?"

"Sips means 'bird' and Sahsapu means 'one who takes quick peeks.' My mama gave me that name because I like to spy and hide out and watch others from a distance. Our names are in the sacred language of the People of the Dawnland. Mihku's name means—"

"Stop!" Mihku interrupted. "She doesn't need to know that!"

"Come on, tell me!" Kessa cupped her hands gently around the little bird and set her down next to Mihku. She stroked the fur on his back, and he looked away shyly.

"Mihku means 'squirrel' and Maskosit means 'smelly feet.' And it's true—I do have smelly feet. I have never, ever known another squirrel with feet as stinky as mine." Mihku hung his head in shame and heaved a sigh.

"I wouldn't get too close if I were you," Sippy said as she fluttered over to the tomato bush and poked her beak into the leaves.

Kessa pulled the other bulky glove from her hand and set it down beside the first one. It was a welcome relief to have her bare hands resting in the cool soil. She spotted a small weed, plucked it out, and tossed it aside.

"It never works with weeds. Weeds don't grow when I touch them—only the herbs and the other plants. I just don't get it."

"Mihku, isn't it time you explained all this to her?" Sippy said as she used her beak to pull a stringy shoot from inside the tangled base of the tomato plant.

"Oh, yes. Well, the way the Gift works with plants is that anything you want to grow, will, and the opposite is true for things you don't want to grow."

"So when I first touched the dill seedling in my house, it grew because I wanted it to thrive? And when I touch weeds, they don't shoot up because I don't want them in my garden?"

"Precisely!" Sippy chirped. "This magic taps into your unconscious, so you don't have to think too hard about it."

"What if I see a patch of wildflowers when I'm with my friends and I want to pick one, but I don't want my friends to see it start growing right in my hands? What then?"

"Same thing," Mihku said. "Simply think that you don't want it to grow. Say it aloud or in your head—either should work just fine as long as you're firm and clear about it." His tail puffed up high and fluffy behind him.

"I don't think that's—" Sippy began, but Kessa cut her off.

"I'll try." She reached her ungloved hands toward the basil and cupped them around the leaves. Mihku and Sippy watched, unmoving, as she gently closed her slender fingers around the leafy stalks. She closed her eyes.

I don't want you to grow right now. Don't grow, don't grow, little plant. She imagined all kinds of plants stunted, unable to lengthen their stems or reach up to the sun. *That should do it! I don't need those silly gloves.* She could feel the leaves tickle against her palms. When she opened her eyes, they were shriveling a bit, drooping and darkening around the edges. She pulled her hands away and took in the sad-looking basil with a sigh.

"Well, it does take some practice." Mihku scurried over to the basil and put his nose into the soil at the base of the stalks. "Maybe you thought about not growing a little too much. Perhaps I was wrong."

"This is why you need me." Sippy hopped forward. "Kessa, like I said, this magic is subtle. It needs a bit of a delicate touch. Just be relaxed and act natural."

"Act natural?" Kessa sputtered. "There is nothing natural about any of this!" Just then, a small whoosh of air grazed her cheek and a flash of wings clipped across her peripheral vision. When Kessa looked upward, she spied the dark outline of Sippy's outstretched wings against the cloudless blue sky.

"Where is she off to in such a hurry?" Kessa said, turning to Mihku, but all she saw was the drooping basil plant and no squirrel in sight. Out across the yard she spotted Arthur first, tromping through the grass with high knees. Not too far behind him, she could make out a jubilant silhouette topped with a wild fluff of hair.

Millie was doing her usual thing, alternately sprinting and leaping as she bounded across the green expanse until close enough to grab ahold of Arthur's hand. For a moment, they were a small paper-doll chain on the horizon. As he yanked her one way, she yanked him the other, a careful cut-out fused at the weakest point, something Kessa might have accidentally ripped apart as a child.

Chapter 15: Big Noises

You couldn't call it the Fourth of July because it always happened after Independence Day, but everyone in the county considered the Green Corn Festival the big event of the summer—including Kessa, who looked forward to seeing the lights explode over the lake each year. The festival usually happened on the third weekend in July, and it was the only time during the summer when Kessa didn't feel like she was out in the middle of nowhere.

People from all over came out to the lake with their canoes and kayaks. They gathered in groups and pitched tents on the many small beaches that surrounded the water. There were bonfires and cookouts and the muddled noises of distant conversation floating by, catching in the huddled rushes of the outermost banks. The murmurs that carried on the breeze late into the night always kept Kessa awake long after her usual bedtime.

"Be back at nine! I'll have the popcorn ready!" her dad called as she made her way to the garden for one last look before the sun set.

When she approached the side yard, she saw Arthur making his way through the tall grass headed her way, without Millie.

"I was hoping I'd find you out here," he said, and then he began speaking so fast that Kessa could only stare, eyebrows raised, as the words tumbled out of his mouth.

"I've got some garden gloves for you—they used to be my mom's, but she doesn't need them anymore, and I thought you might like them. You know, so you don't have to use those big winter gloves. Your hands probably get really sweaty in those." He paused to take a breath, and the faint sound of music coming from a boat somewhere out on the lake hovered on the cool evening breeze that passed between them.

"Oh. Thanks." Kessa took the gloves and draped them over the watering can.

"I want to show you something. Come on!"

"Right now?" She cast a hesitant look toward the house. Her dad would be expecting her back soon.

"Yeah! I've been working on something."

His long legs marched across the green as they headed over to his house while the lake gently swallowed up the last of the sunlight. The "woods"—a small grove of trees that divided their properties—came into view. They followed the path through to the other side, and Kessa soon found that she had to lift her legs high to tramp through the uncut grass.

"Your lawn is getting seriously out of control."

"Yeah, my dad usually does the mowing, but he hasn't been around." Arthur led the way to the back of the yard, which, like hers, sloped down to the lake.

As they approached a massive structure built of sticks and tall branches leaning into each other, Kessa's eyes widened. She had seen many of Arthur's lean-to forts over the years, and this was by far the largest one he had ever made. Small glowing white lights outlined the entrance, with many more tacked up on the inside of the roof as well. Wildflowers had been carefully sown through the tangle of twisting sticks like something out of a woodland fairy wedding.

"Wow," she breathed. The word came on an exhale, an involuntary escape that she caught with the palm of her hand.

"It took me a week to build it. And those are solar lights." Arthur stood before his creation for a moment, hands on hips, beaming at his masterful architecture. Then he got down on his knees and ducked inside. Kessa followed.

They sat side by side as Kessa rested her eyes on the surface of the lake, which was dotted with people out in their canoes to see the fireworks. The sky faded upward into a deepening shade of blue, and she hugged her knees to her chest to squeeze away the chill. Arthur took out a small pocketknife and began peeling the bark off a stick no longer than a ruler.

"What's that?"

"Whittling. I can make it pretty sharp."

"Can I do some?"

"What about your nails?"

Kessa rolled her eyes and grabbed the stick. The knife was extremely sharp, and coils of fresh wood peeled away easily. It was surprisingly relaxing and satisfying to hone the spear. When she had fashioned the point as finely as she could, she pressed her finger to it to test the sharpness. It was something Toria would like. Toria had lots of pointy things, like the pocketknife she had stolen from Maddy's big brother, plucking it from the top of his dresser like it had always been hers, and the liquid liner she used to make sharp little wings at the corners of her eyes. Of course, there were also the points you couldn't see and never knew when they might poke out. Those were the sharpest of all.

"Is this good?"

"Yes," he said, so quietly she almost missed it. But he was not looking at the spear in her hand. He was looking directly at her.

"What? Is there something on my face?" She reflexively swiped her hand across her mouth, and he dropped his head, gave a funny sort of laugh, and smiled at the ground. There was a loud whistle and then a popping noise as the first cracker went off. Kessa handed him the short spear and put down the knife. "I have to get to the porch. They're starting now."

"Or we could watch them from here." He held her gaze, the small glow from the lights reflecting in his eyes like tiny dancing fireflies. "It's the perfect view."

She froze for a moment, not sure what to say, and her heart quickened as she considered the unexpected invitation. "I-I promised my dad I would be back. He's got popcorn. It's just what we usually do." A series of crackling sounds came from somewhere far off on the lake. Dozens of smaller pops and hisses hit the sky as people began lighting their own private fireworks down on the beaches.

"Oh. Okay." He placed the spear beside him like it was made of glass, holding it delicately between his thumb and forefinger and pressing his lips in, as if trying to hold back a mouthful of words. "Well, I guess I'll see you later, then." He used the back of his wrist to swipe the bangs away from his eyes and began whittling a new stick, deliberately and precisely, like any boy would do.

Kessa's heart raced as she marched across the grass under the moon toward her house. Had Arthur wanted her to watch the fireworks in the fort with him? Wasn't that something a boyfriend and girlfriend would do? She bit her lower lip to stop the smile that was threatening to take over her entire face as two more whistles popped in the air and fizzled against the sky, followed by the first very loud boom. The bigger ones were about to start. A dazzling explosion of pink and green and white sparkles rained from the sky, and she broke out into a light run, not wanting to miss the display from the porch.

When she paused at the base of the back staircase to catch her breath, there was another boom, and this one she felt deep within her chest, a sweet thunder that vibrated from her rib cage to her toes. It was a big noise, but the feeling was bigger. She searched her mind for the words to describe it, but all the adjectives flew out into the night and the similes teased her, flickering on and off like lightening bugs quietly escaping to the tops of the trees.

• • •

Kessa sat out in the garden with a bowl of crunchy puffy peanut snacks for Mihku. She expected him to come bolting around the edge of the house as he usually did, but after five minutes, she began to wonder if he would be visiting at all. There was no sign of Sippy either, and the trees, usually bursting with morning bird sounds, were unusually quiet.

She tossed a peanut puff into the grass and called out for Mihku with a few clicks of her tongue. "Mihku? Where are you? I have a snack, and I think you'll really like it!"

After a few minutes, she heard a scrabbling sound. Mihku appeared and started digging in the dirt, looking rather fearful and frazzled.

"There you are!" Kessa smiled and held out her bowl. "Try these! I brought them out just for you."

"Ahhhh!" Mihku jumped into the air and ran back and forth, hugging the edge of the garden, his soft white belly close to the soil. His eyes darted around, and he backed away slowly as Kessa lowered the bowl to the ground.

"What's wrong? Mihku? Are you okay?" She leaned forward with a concerned look and tilted her head to the side as she offered a peanut snack in her outstretched hand.

"The Big Noises—they were here last night." Mihku looked from side to side as if expecting a lightning bolt to come out of nowhere and strike right in the middle of the garden.

"Big noises?"

"Yes! The Big Noises, the ones that ripple through you and set your heart leaping in all directions. They come around the same time every July, but no one is ever prepared for the horror. Ow, ow, my aching ears." Mihku reached his paws up and folded his ears down flat against the sides of his head. "My ears are still ringing. What if my hearing has been permanently damaged?"

"Is this about the fireworks from last night? We have them every July for the Green Corn Festival. It's like a big party."

"Party?" Mihku lowered his paws and looked into Kessa's eyes. "You humans make those noises for . . . for fun?"

"Well, yeah, fireworks are cool. Did you see any of those bright colors exploding over the lake? It's pretty awesome." Kessa bit into a peanut puff with a crunch, happily recalling the beautiful display. "I bet Sippy had the best view of all. Where is she, anyway?"

"No, no, not Sippy. She left the area with her friends last night. I hope she's okay."

"She left? What—you mean because of the fireworks?"

"Yes. It's awful for all the animals, especially the birds. Last year, one of her friends, a jay, got so scared and disoriented from the loud noises that he flew out of his nest and smacked right into a tree. It's a miracle he survived."

"That's awful." Kessa had a sinking feeling in her stomach, like when you first realize that something special, like mermaids or unicorns, might not be real. All those years she had been enjoying the fireworks, they had been disturbing and scaring the wildlife. She thought about Bucky, how he used to run and hide when the fireworks would start to go off.

"It is awful, I'll tell ya. It feels like the end of the world is coming."

"I had no idea," Kessa whispered. She thought for a minute, then nodded. "You know what? I'll write a letter to the mayor. I have some fancy stationery in my craft drawer here that I've been dying to use. I do love the fireworks, but there's got to be another way we can celebrate the Green Corn Festival. Maybe a laser show or something?" Kessa picked up her phone and began tapping out some notes. "I've seen videos of drones doing cool displays too. Even a big bonfire could be fun, with some live music."

"I sure wouldn't mind some music. That probably wouldn't bother the birds too much either." Mihku began munching on a peanut puff, his teeth making little scraping sounds, and then he paused to look up at Kessa, eyes brimming. "I think Nokomis was right to give you the Gift." He put his nose into the bowl and his whiskers twitched wildly. "And I think you were right to bring me these peanut puffs!"

Chapter 16: The Life of a Squirrel

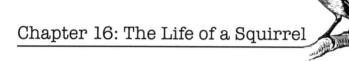

"It's me."

"Hey, Kess! I'm on my way to the mall with Maddy. Maddy, it's Kessa—say hi!"

A knot wriggled in Kessa's stomach, looping and tightening around the feelings that lived there among the acid and bile. Of course they were going to hang out together. It didn't mean anything. Toria was still her best friend, and that wouldn't change. Would it?

"So, what's up? How's the lake? Meet any cute boys?"

"Well, actually, I wanted to talk about that—" There was some muffled laughter, and Maddy said something she couldn't make out. The Latin music that Toria's mom always listened to blared in the background. Though Kessa had been in Spanish Club for two whole years, she couldn't understand a single word.

"Hold on." Toria's voice, coming in clearer and suddenly up close, startled her. "I'm putting you on speaker, okay?"

"Remember that boy who lives close by—Arthur? Well, I think . . . I might have a crush on him." Kessa had to hold the phone away from her ear because Toria and Maddy burst into shrieks, followed by a litany of unsuppressed giggles.

"I can't believe our little Kessa finally has a crush!"

"I think I'm going to ask him to go on a hike with me. It's perfect because he got me a compass for my birthday, and I really want to learn how to use it."

"Go for it, Kessa!" Maddy shouted over the rolling bachata beats.

"So, if I ask him to go on a hike, does that mean it's a date?"

"Do you want it to be a date?" Toria half asked, half yelled before crooning along to the next verse.

Kessa waited for her to finish, not wanting to be cut off by the refrain. "I'm not sure. I just want to spend time with him. I don't want things to change between us, though. I mean, I do ... but I don't. Does that make sense?"

"Everything is always changing all the time. Just do something. Better to be the wind than a cloud, ya know?" The music faded at the end of the song. "Remember, you have Mars in Aries, Kess. Use it. You gotta tap into that."

"Mars in Aries?"

"Did you not read those astro-chart descriptions I emailed to you?"

There was an odd quiet on the line, and Kessa swore she could hear the hollow smack of bubblegum popping against the roof of Toria's mouth.

"I just forgot. You know I hardly ever check my email." Another track began to play and Kessa heard Toria ask her mom to turn it up. She hung up the phone and headed out to the garden, her face tilted up at the sky. Puffy or wispy, it wasn't so bad to be a cloud, so long as the wind was easy. Clouds got to change colors with the sunsets and drift past stars at night. They were the keepers of secrets and daydreams and a place to rest your eyes when the sky was too vast and blue. But now her mind lowered to the earth because she needed to figure out what was going on with the garden.

The basil, mint, cilantro, and parsley all looked like they had been feasted on again. She knelt down and ran her ungloved fingers across the tops of the plants. She had been having to do this every morning for a few days now and was beginning to wonder if her plants would ever grow on their own without her touch. Something was grazing on the herbs before they even had a chance to flourish. Her gift couldn't be meant only to grow food for hungry creatures by the lake, and if it was, she didn't want it to be.

Mihku darted out from beneath the great rhododendron bush by the side of the house. "I know what to do!" His tail twitched and shivered as he surveyed the garden. "Marigolds! Rabbits. Hate. Marigolds."

"How do you know it's rabbits? I mean, aren't there many different animals that could eat this stuff?" Kessa raised an eyebrow.

"It's not me, Kessa, I swear. I would never. I'm not much of a salad guy anyway."

"So, if it is rabbits, you really think marigolds will keep them away? Why wouldn't they just go around them if they didn't like them?"

"I don't know," Mihku said, "but that's what Azeban said, and he knows a lot about this kind of thing. I stayed up really late last night, so I did get to talk to him, but boy am I tired." He yawned.

"Okay, I guess I'll have to get some marigolds. If you really think it will work."

"Of course it will work!" Mihku shouted. "Azeban is smart. We can trust his advice."

Kessa gave a little half smile. "I guess it's too bad Azeban isn't my animal guide, then," she said wryly.

"Azeban? Please. He wouldn't be caught dead talking to humans. Going through their trash? Maybe. But talking to them? No, definitely not! Besides, he only comes out when the sky is dark, well past bedtime."

"I was only kidding." Kessa shook her head and ran her hand over the parsley again. The curly leaves began to rustle as if touched by a sudden breeze, and two new shoots broke through the soil.

"Hey, Kess! We are leaving in five minutes!" her dad called from the porch. Mihku froze in place, still as a statue.

"It's okay—he's just letting Bucky out. I'm going to visit my friend Ruth today. She owns an animal sanctuary. I usually go whenever I can when I'm here for the summer."

Mihku relaxed and looked around furtively. "I'd better get going. I just got a tip about a beech tree a few miles away from here. Beechnuts are ideal for gnawing." He showed his two long front teeth.

"A tip?" Kessa looked around. "Who told you about the beechnuts?"

"Probably someone in my family. We look out for each other the same way plants do."

"Plants look out for each other?" Kessa touched one of the new green tomatoes on the vine and watched it blush into a ruddy-orange color. "That's amazing."

Mihku suddenly thrust his nose to the sky and closed his eyes. "Ooh, looks like there will be a good harvest this fall! I better get over there and check it out."

"You can see it?" Kessa remarked, her eyes growing wide.

"Of course! I didn't realize it until just now, but you probably don't even know you have this ability too. I'll show you. Just close your eyes and focus on the light and darkness behind your eyelids. Don't think about anything in particular."

Kessa closed her eyes and couldn't see anything but the usual amorphous blobs of light and dark patches. She squinched up her whole face and forced her eyes to close tighter, but still there was nothing. "I don't see anything." She opened them up, and Mihku was nowhere to be found. "Mihku! You said you would teach me!"

She stood up and was walking toward the front of the house when an image of tall plants and trees interrupted her thoughts. She stopped in her tracks and looked off toward the garden, but her eyes were not focused on anything. A dizzying, rushing sensation took hold as a few more images flashed through her mind.

Her heart no longer had individual beats; it was one continuous humming vibration, and she could smell the earth as if her nose were stuck right into a patch of freshly raked soil and old leaves. When she closed her eyes, she was no longer standing on the lawn but looking up into a grove of trees. The trees were taller than she had ever seen before, and bright sunlight was pouring down through the branches high above. She was hit with the strong scent of pine needles, and then the rocks and giant leaves beside her face began to rush away as if a low, very swift wind was carrying her across the ground. It was the quick and marvelous life of a squirrel.

The car door slammed shut and startled Kessa from the vision. "Kessa, let's go. I've got the air-conditioning on!" her dad shouted in his impatient way, as if cooled air couldn't be wasted for even a second.

"There in a minute!" she yelled back.

Kessa reached into her back pocket for her phone and pulled up the notes app. There was too much she would forget if she didn't write it down. No time for flowery adjectives—she just needed to get it all out. She began walking briskly toward the car as she tapped at her phone. Even the clouds seemed to understand: it was a good time to move like the wind.

Chapter 17: Ruth

As her dad parked the car in the large patch of dirt at the end of the driveaway, Kessa peered out the window at the old carved wooden sign for Pennacook Pines Animal Sanctuary. She had been visiting the sanctuary since she was just a toddler, Daisy's age. No other cars were in the small lot, which meant there were probably not any other volunteers for the day. She could understand why: as she got out of the air-conditioned car, the heat closed around her like an unwelcome hug.

Kessa left her dad at the picnic table under the tree with his laptop and Bucky melting into the shade. She skipped up the path to go find Ruth, who was usually engaged in chores somewhere between the greenhouse down the hill on the left and the broad pasture that stretched out on the right of the barn. A large expanse of dirt and rubble led up to the barn's entrance, and Kessa was glad she had remembered to wear her old boots. They usually needed a good hosing down after a day of stomping around the sanctuary.

Out in the field beside the barn, Kessa immediately spotted the retired carriage horses, Rig and Willa, and then her eyes drifted over to a new animal far off on the green. It was a cow or bull that she hadn't seen before. A brief twinge of excitement dissolved into cautious wonder. Every time someone new arrived at the sanctuary, there was always the possibility of a sad backstory.

Kessa poked her head into the barn and walked inside. The dark coolness was a welcome relief, and even the earthy smell of hay and manure was a comfort that embraced her like a familiar friend. Kessa spotted the goats—Baxter, Tiny, and Pepper, who had no doubt come inside to seek the shade—and her favorite sheep, Gordy, who was lingering in the back door with his fluffy backside facing her.

"Hey, Gordy. Could you move, fella? I'm looking for Ruth." Gordy wouldn't budge. He stared out into the sunshine as Kessa squeezed past him, running her hand over his bushy body as she did so.

The back of the barn looked out over a gentle slope of green land that ended with a willow-tree-shaded pond at the bottom of the hill. The pond was only a fraction of the size of Lake Wabanaki, and Kessa had always adored it. When Kessa was six, Ruth said she could call it anything she wanted to, so Kessa had named it Jewel Pond.

As a little girl, and even now, it seemed magical to her, like something out of a fairy tale, with all of its lily pads and pussy willows, its damp green smell tickling her nostrils like tendrils of ancient mermaid hair. She had watched countless frogs peek out from among the tall grass and even wondered, at one point, if one of them might have been a prince. But it didn't matter if she kissed a frog or not, because she felt like a princess whenever she was there, dipping her toes in and letting her heels melt into the ripples on the surface of the water.

Now, with the sun reaching noon heights, Jewel Pond looked stunning beneath the huge willow tree that reached out over it, its lazy green fronds dripping into the still water. As she gazed at her favorite shady spot and remembered how lovely it was to dip her toes in the water a loud racket of honking arose from behind the shed on the right, shattering the serene moment.

Kessa recognized the sound of geese, but she didn't remember the sanctuary having any. She walked out further onto the dirt path and saw a large gaggle of gray-and-white geese waddling toward her, honking and hollering all the while. As they came nearer, she stepped back and eyed them as they made their way down to the pond, their bodies like little bobbing buoys on the rolling green.

One of the last geese, a white one with gray patches on its wings, stopped and stared at her. Kessa locked eyes with it and instantly felt a jolt zap through her body. Her vision went blurry. There was a great lurching sensation, and then all she could see was broken glass and bars slicing through her view as she tumbled across a stretch of road, the smell of hot tarmac stinging in her nose. The screeching of tires and panicked honking filled her with terror. Sirens rang in her ears, and she felt she might throw up right then and there. She wanted to get away, but she was trapped, her frantic wings pressed against the box.

"Kessa?"

A kind voice broke the trance, and Kessa found herself sitting in the middle of the pathway. She couldn't understand why she was on the ground. Had she just passed out? Ruth was wearing thick rubber gloves, and strands of black and gray hair from her long braid were coming loose around her face.

"I see you have met the geese," she said. The lines around her eyes were like deeply etched whiskers drawn over her broad cheekbones. She squinted into the sun and studied the geese, now happily swimming around the pond.

Kessa didn't know what to say. She wasn't sure what she had just experienced, but it seemed similar to the vision Mihku had shown her earlier of a squirrel's life. But this time, the vision had been far less pleasant, if not downright terrifying. "There's a lot of them," she said as Ruth offered her hand and helped Kessa to her feet.

"Yes. I'll need help naming them all." She smiled and gestured toward the pond. "Let's go sit under the willow, and I'll tell you about our new friends."

As they walked down the hill, the wet, earthy smell of the pond mingled with the scent of the purple lupines on the meadow's slope. Kessa climbed onto the flat outcropping of rock beside the water. It was the ideal picnic spot— it was shaded by the willow and was also close enough to the water so that you could dip your toes in if you wanted to—but Kessa wasn't the least bit hungry. She was still a bit sick and woozy from what had happened outside the barn. Like with Mihku, she knew she had received some kind of communication from that goose, but she didn't know what to make of it. Her eyes roved over the swimming birds, looking for the one that had made eye contact with her, but with their similar coloring, not one of them stood out.

Ruth took off her thick work gloves and placed them on the stone beside her. "Would you like to know what happened to them?" She put a hand on Kessa's shoulder, her kind amber eyes like pools of warm honey as she patiently waited for Kessa's reply.

Kessa breathed in sharply and looked back out over the pond. She recalled the horrible squeal of tires and the frantic feeling of wings pressing against metal bars. She drew her legs in up to her chest and hugged her knees. "Okay," she said, taking a deep breath.

Ruth nodded solemnly. "They were on their way to slaughter from where they had been raised on a poultry farm. The driver of the truck hit a car on the highway. It was a colossal collision, but both drivers survived. The woman in the car made a deal with the truck driver: if she could bring all the geese to safety, she would not press charges. That's how they all ended up here. That very kind woman had once visited my sanctuary as a young girl, so she contacted me."

"I didn't even know that people eat geese." Kessa marveled at the peaceful creatures idling serenely on the pond. How could anyone look at living, breathing animals and see food? She knew Ruth felt the same way, because Ruth was also vegan. Kessa was grateful for the sanctuary and how one woman's compassion had allowed the geese to live.

She turned to Ruth, studying her deeply tanned and creased face for a moment, and then softly thanked her. "I've never passed out like that before. I'm glad you found me when it happened."

"Think nothing of it, my dear. I'm sure it was just a fluke. Perhaps you just need to adjust to this summer heat. And by the way . . ." She reached into the worn bag on her hip, pulled out a small object wrapped in yellow tissue paper with a thin red ribbon, and handed it to her. "Happy birthday, my dear."

"Oh, you didn't have to . . ."

"Ah, but I did. And this is a very important present. I've been waiting many years to pass this on to you."

Kessa felt the weight of the gift and turned it over in her hands. She pulled the red ribbon and carefully tore away the crinkled tissue paper. It looked like a stone carving of a turtle with a few extra round feet, or a person with a large belly. She ran her thumb over its smooth, lumpy formations.

"There are only a few places in the world where these special stones can be found. This one is from the Harricana River in Canada. Harricana comes from the Algonquin name Nanikana, which some say means 'river of biscuits,' referring to these peculiar, smooth formations. Some people call them fairy stones or turtle stones, but my ascendants, the Algonquin people, called them spirit stones and carried them for good luck and protection."

"This isn't a carving?"

"No, this is how they naturally form. They grow those puffy, rounded concretions when lying face down in the clay. The tops get smoothed, over time, by glaciers and water. To look at one in the mud, you would think it was just an ordinary stone, but turn it over, and a unique sculpture is revealed. You see"—

she turned the stone over in Kessa's palm so the flat side faced up—"there are no two alike. As a young lady, my grandmother found one that looked like a pregnant woman with a baby in her belly. She went on to have seven children."

Kessa looked at Ruth and held out the stone. "I can't take this from you. It's too special."

Ruth closed Kessa's fingers around the stone and wrapped her own warm, smooth, and wrinkled hands around Kessa's, then turned her face up to the willow tree. She closed her eyes and smiled, nodding as if she agreed with more than the boughs above her. "No, this was meant to be yours."

. . .

At noon, Ruth brought out some of her famous chickpea salad sandwiches and lemonade, and they joined Kessa's dad for lunch at the picnic table. Kessa wanted to meet the new bull in the pasture right away, but Ruth said he was still shy and needed some space. After eating, they headed over to the chickens' area, where Kessa helped collect eggs to be ground up into their feed. She wanted to talk more about the strange vision with the geese and wondered if Ruth also knew about her ability to make plants grow, but Ruth worked quietly and seemed not to be in a talking mood. Finally, when the sweat and heat were almost too much to bear, Ruth handed Kessa a water bottle and told her to take a break and meet her in the greenhouse before heading back home.

Ruth was waiting with a small bucket and picking little yellow tomatoes from a hanging plant. They were Kessa's favorite, and every summer she looked forward to popping them in her mouth, their tart sweetness breaking against the back of her tongue. Ruth called them Tumbling Toms.

"Thank you for helping me," Ruth said as she handed her the bucket of sweet tomatoes. "We can talk more at your next visit. There was just so much work to be done today, and I have not had any volunteers this week."

Kessa nodded, reaching into her pocket and closing her fingers around her new gift. It already felt familiar against her palm.

"I have something else for you before you go." Ruth went down to the metal table at the end of the greenhouse and came back with two large pots of marigolds. "I'll help you carry these to the car." She strode ahead, and Kessa hurried to follow her out.

"Marigolds! I needed some of those for my garden," Kessa exclaimed. "To keep the rabbits away."

"Of course!" Ruth turned around and gave her a little smile.

Kessa reached into her pocket and rubbed her thumb over the special rock that Ruth had given her, as if the very action could iron away all the swirling questions on her mind and ease the nagging feelings she couldn't put a voice to, the ones that left a prickly feeling somewhere far at the back of her throat.

Chapter 18: Wild Jellyfish

The early morning had been warm, damp, and humming with crickets when Kessa had first woken up, and the temperature was still rising. The late-July sun was already baking her skin, the dew point closing around her like a wet blanket. How could Mihku bare it with all that thick fur?

"It actually keeps me really cool!" Mihku replied before Kessa even opened her mouth.

She stared down at him as he dug furiously in the dirt beside the marigolds, and she sighed. Most of the plants were still being chewed to stubs. There had to be another way to keep the rabbits out. Perhaps it was time for a fence.

"No, we don't need a fence!" Mihku cried. "Azeban said that will only encourage them. The rabbits we have around here are very bold. He told me the best way to deter rabbits is with dog food. Rabbits hate dog food! Besides, if you put up a fence, then how will I get in? I have started several secret stashes in here. I'm going to start keeping my stores under the marigolds."

"Wait, hold up! Dog food? You've got to be kidding me!" Kessa knelt down and ran her hand over the chewed-up basil and a particularly ragged-looking mint plant. They shot up a few inches but seemed much less vigorous than before, as if they were tired and worn out from the seemingly never-ending cycle of being munched on and then revived. The basil plant, which was no longer bushy, had been partially dug up, and new tomatoes disappeared from the vine before they had the chance to ripen.

"I think my growing power is beginning to wear out," Kessa said, frowning as she gently coaxed a yellowing tomato leaf into a deep green. But before she could move on to the next one, it paled back to a sallow yellow. Even running her thumbs directly over the vines didn't seem to do much for the struggling young plants.

"Well, roots store energy. If they are constantly being depleted, it's going to be really tough to keep them in good shape, even with a powerful gift like yours. I say we try the dog food."

"I mean, I guess? It just seems like a weird thing to do. Are you sure Azeban knows what he's talking about?"

"Of course he does!" Mihku scoffed. "These rabbits are difficult and tenacious. He knows how to outsmart all kinds of creatures. We would be foolish not to listen to his advice."

"Okay, well, it's getting hot. I'll put the dog food out later, I promise." Kessa tapped Mihku gently on the forehead with her index finger and then headed for the house, while he continued to dig holes in the garden.

As the screen door banged behind her, Kessa shook off her sandals and wound her ponytail into a shaggy bun atop her head. The coolness the house had previously held was beginning to dissipate, and the muggy air was taking over. She clicked on the rotating fan and pointed it at the writing nook, where she sat down, turned on her phone, and added Arthur's name and number to her contact list. She had always known his number by heart from years of dialing it on the landline, but this was the first time she had saved it to her cell. *Just make the call. It's no big deal. It's just Arthur.*

"Oui, bonjour."

"Oh, hi, Millie. Is Arthur there?"

"Why?"

"Ah, no reason. Just seeing what's up."

"Don't you want to talk to me?"

"Millie, can you just get Arthur?"

"He's in his room, and I don't want to go all the way up there right now."

"Fine, I'll just come over, then." Millie was really starting to get on her nerves.

"Fine. Do what you want. Au revoir."

Maybe going over would be less formal, more natural. She would just say that she was going to go on a hike and if he wanted to join her, he could. If he didn't, then she would just go swimming in the lake or work on her story. Easy. No big deal.

Kessa walked through the living room but paused at the couch where Bucky lay. "Bucky?" He didn't pick up his head like he usually did when someone entered the room. He was typically pretty lazy on humid days, so she went and got him some water from the kitchen sink and put the dish on the floor next to his stool.

"Oh, thank you, dear." Bucky opened his tired watery eyes to half-mast, and Kessa nodded at him with a look of concern. She ran her hand over his coat and felt the quick rise and fall of his breath.

"You just stay here and relax. I'm going out for a bit. Do you want me to let you outside to pee before I go?"

"Oh no, no thank you. I'm just going to take a little nap right now." Bucky closed his eyes again. "If you wouldn't mind bringing that water dish up for me for a moment. . . that would be nice."

"Oh! Yes, of course." Kessa held the dish up for Bucky and he lapped the water. "I'll take you down to the lake when I get back later, okay?"

Kessa tiptoed out of the living room and padded up the stairs to her room. She needed to get dressed properly for the hike. After changing into shorts and a loose T-shirt, she went to the kitchen to fetch the tube of mineral sunscreen her mom had made her pack. Her dad was sitting at the table with the paper, eating a bowl of cereal.

"You know, I really like this almond milk. Fewer calories too," her dad said, crunching a mouthful of cornflakes. "Not that it will make much of a difference." He chuckled and patted his soft, round stomach.

"I told you," Kessa said, smiling to herself. "It's better in every way." She put her foot up on the kitchen chair and began rubbing the sunscreen on her lower leg.

"Where are you going?"

"To Arthur and Millie's. We might go on a hike."

"Really!" He brought the bowl to his lips before saying, "I thought Millie hated hikes."

"Well, I'm thinking maybe just Arthur and I will go."

"Oh." He slurped up the rest of the milk and gave her a funny, lopsided smile. "That compass was a very nice gift. This will be the perfect chance to try it out."

"Yeah. That's what I was thinking." She rubbed the sunscreen into her arms and then applied a blob to her forehead. She hated putting it on her face. It was goopy and always left white smears no matter how much she tried to rub it in.

"Oh, um, Dad? You should keep an eye on Bucky while I'm gone. He seems . . . not great today." Kessa wiped the remaining sunscreen from her sticky palms onto the back of her neck while her dad filled up a water bottle for her at the sink. "I had to help him drink his water."

"Yes, I think he might have some trouble seeing where it is. I've got an appointment with the vet to deal with his glaucoma. He needs eye surgery soon or he could go blind—in fact, he may already have lost a good bit of his sight. I'll check on him after I take my shower."

"Blind? I didn't know it was that bad."

"Unfortunately yes. The surgery could help retain some of his vision, though since he's so old, the vet is a little hesitant about putting him under anesthesia."

"Why? They should just do it! Bucky needs to see."

Kessa filled her pockets with dog food to sprinkle throughout the garden on her way out and grabbed a package of vegan gummies for Millie. Her dad handed her the water bottle and told her to be careful and that if she wasn't back in three hours, he would be looking for her. Though they were familiar with most of the paths surrounding the lake, she promised to call before they left to tell him what trail they would be taking.

As she sat down to put on her hiking boots, she caught a glimpse of herself in the full-length hall mirror. There were white streaks all over her face. Small cuts adorned her knobby knees from where she had tried to shave her legs the other day. If Toria had been going on a hike with a boy, she would have dressed very differently. Kessa smiled at the thought of Toria trying to hobble through the wilderness in her high-heeled sandals, makeup melting off her face in the heat. Kessa finished lacing up her boots and stood in front of the mirror.

Well, it might not be the cutest outfit ever, but at least it's practical.

• • •

Kessa had become used to entering Arthur and Millie's house by going through the side window, and she deftly hopped onto the stool against the outer wall and parted the curtains inside the screen-less opening. Daisy immediately ran over to greet her.

"Kissy! Kissy!" Daisy's hands, like usual, were coated in something sticky. She grabbed the sides of Kessa's face as she scooped her up for a hug.

"It's Kessy, not Kissy, silly!" Kessa kissed her plump cheek, which made Daisy break out into an adorable grin, her tongue poking out between her teeth.

"Kissy kiss Dizzy! Dizzy kiss Kissy!" Daisy kissed Kessa on the cheek, then laughed and kicked her legs, letting Kessa know that she wanted to be put back down. There were a few empty juice boxes and little straws on the floor next to the couch. Daisy squatted over the boxes and tried to poke a chewed-up straw through one of the small holes.

"It looks like you're going on a hike. Is that why you're here?" Millie stood in the hallway, glaring at her. She had a purple stain around her mouth and all over the front of her shirt, looking not unlike she had been attacked by several large grape popsicles.

"Maybe." Kessa folded her arms and raised her eyebrows at Millie, then suddenly remembered she had something in her bag for the gatekeeper. "I brought you something, though!"

Millie took a few hesitant steps forward. "What is it?"

Kessa held out the snack-sized package filled with vegan gummy worms and smiled. "These are for you!"

"I thought gummy stuff had gelatin in it."

"They're vegan ones. All kinds of gummy stuff can be made vegan. Even marshmallows—I have them at home all the time."

"Oh." Millie snatched the bag and looked at the ingredients on the back of the package. "I used to think gelatin was made from jellyfish. Obviously, I know that's not true now. It's a good thing there is vegan gelatin, because real gelatin is dégoûtant. Thinking about all those crushed-up horse hooves makes me really sad and grossed out." Millie shuddered. "And just so you know, I don't want to go on your stupid hike."

"Okay. Fine." Kessa shook her head and started up the stairs.

"But we could do beads." Millie threw the words out like an auctioneer. "Do you want to make a bracelet with me? I have glow-in-the-dark ones, pink ones, and opal."

Kessa paused on the stairs and mustered up a sympathetic look. "Maybe later, okay?"

Millie tilted her head to the side, held a gummy worm between her teeth, and stretched it until it snapped. Kessa gripped the banister and turned away from the unnerving pressure of Millie's gaze.

"Do you know what a shebang is?"

Kessa let out an audible sigh. "No, Millie, I don't," she said, trying to creep away from the conversation by inching up another stair.

"I heard Candice talking about me on the phone today. She said, 'One day that flame is gonna set fire to the whole shebang.' I knew she was talking about me because that's what she calls me sometimes—Li'l Flame." Millie pointed at her hair and then loaded another gummy worm between her teeth. "You'll be sorry you didn't do beads with me because I was going to share my rare ones," she said while chewing and smacking on her mouthful of worms. "You'll be sorry. Next time, they'll be used up. They'll all be gone."

. . .

The stairs creaked with each step, and Kessa pinched her nose when she got to the second floor. Millie's room had a strange smell, and you could kind of get a whiff of it from the top of the stairs. It was the ripe smell of dirty laundry mixed with the rank yet slightly sweet smell of decaying food. The odor of neglected damp towels was very distinctly coming from the bathroom on her right, and as she approached Millie's room, Kessa clasped a hand over her mouth and poked her head through the doorway.

It was impossible to make out the floor, as there was a great sprawling network of blanket forts that somehow seemed to also encompass the bed. A small rotating fan hummed from a cluttered desktop in the far corner, and a long extension cord snaked from below the open window and disappeared behind the desk. Between the desk and the wall, a pile of books threatened to avalanche into the sheet that was drawn taut between a bookshelf and a large bureau, where one sheet corner was closed into the top drawer. Kessa grimaced and moved on to Arthur's room at the end of the hall. The door was closed and a sign that said "Please Knock" was hung neatly from a single nail that protruded from the center.

She paused before the door. She hadn't been totally alone with Arthur since the night of the fireworks, and thinking about it made her heart race. But this was just a hike, like she'd gone on countless times in the past—not a date. Or was it? Kessa swallowed and gave a tentative knock.

"Millie, I told you to stay out!"

"It's not Millie. It's me, Kessa."

"Oh." Arthur opened the door and stood there for a moment with a look on his face like he was trying to do a complex math problem without any paper. Then he moved out of the way and held his arm out for her to enter, bowing his head a bit as if ushering in a noble presence.

Arthur's bed held an old quilt, but it was neatly spread and tucked up tightly. Something on the bedside table caught her eye right away. It was the short spear she had honed in the fort the night of the fireworks. He had made countless spears of his own, but he had kept hers. Had he thought it special in some way? The thought caused a small catch in her breath.

His room looked the same as she had seen it last, if not a tad neater. The tall bookshelf beside the window was well organized with his many survival guides and an entire encyclopedia set that took up the bottom three shelves. Milk crates on either side of the closet held other creative endeavors, materials, and curious collections of shells, rocks, and other artifacts from nature like bird nests. And much to Kessa's relief, she could breathe through her nose, as Arthur's room held no foul smells. The pleasant scent of pine and cedar wafted up from the closed chest at the foot of the bed, where she took a seat.

"I was thinking—maybe we could go on a hike today?"

"Right now?"

"Sure."

"I don't know. It's really hot out. I'm not sure you can handle it."

"Can you?"

He grinned at her. "I've hiked in a lot worse."

Kessa laughed. "I know. I remember last summer when you got caught out in the rainstorm—you came back totally covered in mud!"

"You wouldn't go with me that time, though. I guess it was a good thing you didn't." His grin faded, and he lowered his eyes to her hiking boots for a moment before snapping his fingers. He quickly grabbed a compass from a small drawer in his desk and tucked a folded-up map into the back pocket of his faded cargo pants. "Did you bring that compass I got for you?"

"Yeah, it's in my bag," she said, patting the front pocket.

Arthur opened his closet to get his shoes, but just before he stuck his head in, Kessa caught a small, closed-mouth smile spread across his face. She put a hand to her chest, where it felt like a wild jellyfish was suddenly leaping around where her heart was supposed to be.

Chapter 19: Fun Guy

As they picked their way through the forest along the well-worn path, any nervousness Kessa had felt before about being alone with Arthur melted away. The conversation flowed from one topic to the next, sprinkled with silly oddball jokes that always got them laughing and punctuated here and there with more serious, rambling thoughts. It was just as easy between them as it had always been. She talked about her last visit to the sanctuary, how the geese came to Pennacook Pines, and the special stone that Ruth had given her. Arthur nodded and listened intently. He said he knew all about spirit stones and where they could be found.

"Hey, you should come with me next time," Kessa said. "My dad is taking me again next week."

"I'd really like to. I haven't been in a while. I'm sure my mom wouldn't mind, but Millie will probably want to come along—you know how she is."

"Oh, I don't mind if she comes. My dad has enough room in the car—if he doesn't bring Bucky, that is."

"You don't?" A look crossed his face like he was physically pained by her reply. He sat on a fallen birch and chugged from his water bottle. His bangs were now drenched with sweat and sticking to his forehead, and Kessa, like a limp wet rag, collapsed next to him on the log. Her own water bottle was nearly empty, and they still had the entire journey back ahead of them. Though it had taken them an hour to hike up to where they were, Arthur had explained that they were going to cut through to a smaller trail and take a different way home. Kessa picked away at the peeling white bark and waited for him to finish his drink.

"We're at the halfway point now. Here, I'll show you." Arthur unfolded the map across his knees and placed the compass on top of it. Kessa pulled out hers and eyed the creased paper, not having any idea where they were or what she was supposed to do with the compass. Arthur talked for a few minutes about how it worked and explained the difference between magnetic north and true north and something called declination.

"Pretty cool, huh?" Arthur looked up at Kessa and she nodded.

"Er, I think I just need a little practice." She was determined to prove to Arthur that she could get the hang of it, and by the time they were halfway down the rapidly disappearing path, she really was beginning to feel more confident. It was kind of exciting being on an unmarked trail and relying on the compass for direction. She usually just followed Arthur when they went on hikes, but now she felt like they were working together to figure out the way home.

Soon, there was hardly any trail to speak of, and it started to get dicey, as there were many fallen trees and dense wooded patches that took a bit of careful footwork to manage. When Kessa looked down at her compass again, she almost tripped over a massive tangle of vines. As she bent over to dislodge her foot, she noticed what looked like a small white nubby snowball nestled in the moss at the base of a tree.

Fascinated, she reached out to touch it, and it suddenly ballooned to the size of a small melon beneath her palm. She snatched her hand back and whipped her head around to see if

Arthur had seen what she had done to the weird mushroom ball. She met his startled green eyes with a stutter.

"I, uh—what is this thing?" She stood up and tried to act as though nothing strange had happened while Arthur stooped down to stare at the odd-looking fungus.

"This is the biggest Lycoperdon I've ever seen! I've never found one larger than three inches around before. This thing is a monster!"

"Lyco what?"

"Lycoperdon perlatum." Arthur ran his fingers over the bumpy white surface of the giant mushroom. "Most people just call them puffballs, but they're also known as warted puffballs, gem-studded puffballs, and for some weird reason, the devil's snuff-box."

Kessa felt relief wash over her as she realized that Arthur probably hadn't seen the thing actually expand. She wiped her sweaty palms on the sides of her shorts and cleared her throat. "It's really weird. I've never seen one before."

"Yeah, and you know what else is awesome about it?" His mouth twitched up at the corner, and then broke into a full grin.

"What?"

"The genus name Lycoperdun literally translates to 'wolf fart.'"

Kessa was still laughing as they continued on through the forest. "Dad's never going to believe me when I tell him I ran into a wolf fart on our hike." She recalled what Mihku had said about plants communicating with each other, and she wondered what the puffballs would say if they could talk.

"Hey." Arthur looked back at Kessa and said, "Why does Ms. Mushroom go out with Mr. Mushroom?"

"Why?"

"Because he's a fun guy!" Arthur looked over his shoulder again, flashing his stretchy grin, and Kessa stumbled a bit. "Get it? Fungi?"

She indulged him with a single raised eyebrow, and they marched onward, quiet but for the sound of their boots crushing the earth below. Kessa paid attention to her breath and focused on the ground so she wouldn't trip. Every now and then, she pushed branches or vines away carefully so they wouldn't suddenly grow longer or wither and die.

She was getting better at controlling how her touch affected plants, but she had to be thoughtful about it and focus on keeping her mind in a relaxed sort of state, just as Sippy had said. Act natural. For a fleeting moment, she thought of telling Arthur about her abilities, about the Gift, but she decided to ask him something else instead.

"You probably know something about this, and I was wondering if it's true that plants can talk—"

"To each other? Yeah!" Arthur cut her off enthusiastically and suddenly became very animated. "They communicate by sending chemicals through the air and into underground fungal networks within the soil. They even help protect their direct offspring. Trees have families just like people do."

"That's pretty cool."

"It's amazing. Some plants when under attack can send out chemical distress calls that will attract the natural predators of whatever is attacking them to come to the rescue." Arthur stopped abruptly in his tracks and turned toward Kessa. "I bet you're thinking, if I love plants so much, then why do I eat them? Right?" He grinned and gave her boot a playful kick in the toe.

Kessa folded her arms across her chest. "Actually, I was wondering how much farther until we're out of here."

His eyes gleamed mischievously, giving a nice sparkle to the woody green of his irises. "Why? Do you want our adventure to be over?"

She rolled her eyes. "You're not planning on getting us lost, are you?"

"I would never let anything bad happen to you. You know that, right?" He locked eyes with her and jammed his thumb toward the large bag on his back. "I never go into the woods without a hatchet, steel, flint, and rope."

Kessa allowed a closed-mouthed smile and tilted her head. "Are you trying to sound like a survival nerd?"

"There is nothing nerdy about being prepared," he said, a slow grin tugging at the corners of his mouth.

"Just to be clear, I don't need anyone to save me. I can slay my own dragons."

"Whoa, hang on now. Who said anything about dragons?"

She struggled to hold in another burgeoning smile and tried to think of something to say. The way they were talking now felt different from their usual teasing. She'd seen it on TV shows and in movies, and she knew you were supposed to say something witty and quick and somehow remain calm and cool on the surface regardless of how tangled up you might feel on the inside. Toria would probably know exactly what to say in a situation like this, her clever tongue wrapped in syrup and barbed wire.

"You're right, it's good to be prepared, which is why I'm thankful you've brought so much water," she chirped as she unscrewed the top to her water bottle. "And since you have so kindly shown interest in my safety, you should know that dehydration would be a major threat to my survival, so . . . hand over your water, please." Kessa briefly pressed her eyes closed and held out her water bottle.

"You're really something else, you know that, Kessa Caliper? Really something else."

Arthur clinked his container to hers and proceeded to pour half of the remaining water from his canteen into her open plastic bottle. Though warm, and bearing a distinctly metallic taste, it quenched her thirst more than any drink ever had.

Chapter 20: Lola

"There's just one stop we need to make before we head back home," Arthur said as they came to the bottom of the hiking trail and stepped out from the thicket.

"Really?" Kessa could barely hide her exhaustion. All she wanted to do was get home, peel out of her damp clothes, and jump into the lake.

"There's someone I want you to meet."

Kessa's face twisted in horror as she swiped at the sweat on her upper lip, but Arthur just smiled and led her into what looked like somebody's backyard. A small red house perched on the upslope of the green, and it had a deck that was built out over a tiny fenced-in area. As they drew closer, she could make out an animal sitting in the small slice of shade cast by the house. The creature looked like a giant poodle with a long neck.

They stopped at a tree, and Arthur told her to stand behind it. He dashed along the edge of the woods beside the house while she stood and stared at the animal, trying to figure out what it was.

"The old man is gone—his car isn't in the drive, so I think it's safe." He grabbed Kessa by the hand and pulled her along.

"Is that a camel? A sheep? What is that thing?"

Arthur whistled as he approached the fence of the animal's pen, and it turned to look at them. It wasn't a dog or a camel or a sheep. It was . . .

"An alpaca!" Arthur said as he poked his nose through the fence. "Isn't she adorable?"

She was probably one of the cutest things Kessa had ever seen, but Kessa didn't say anything. She just stared at Arthur as he began to scale the fence. "What are you doing?!"

"I'm visiting Lola," he said, jumping down from the fence and into the pen. "That's what I named her. She doesn't have any friends, and alpacas can get lonely, since they're herd animals. She should be with at least one other alpaca, but I'm just trying to keep her company as best I can. She seems depressed lately."

Kessa leaned into the fence and watched Arthur pet Lola's huge fluffy back. "How can she tolerate this heat with all that wool on her?" Without warning, Lola jerked her head forward, rose up on all fours, and trotted right over to where Kessa stood.

"Hey! She likes you." Arthur laughed. "I told you she needed some friends!"

Kessa reached through the fence and stroked Lola's neck. Instantly, a powerful heat rushed through Kessa. Her neck and ears had been hot before, but now she was boiling. Was her skin going to melt off? She gripped the fence to keep from collapsing. Maybe it was heatstroke.

Lola's lower lip quivered, and then the alpaca, too, leaned into the fence, before slowly lowering her head to the ground.

"There's something wrong with her," Arthur said. He gently pulled the overhanging bushy wool away from her eyes.

"It's heat stress. The old man leaves me out in the sun all day, and I don't think I can take it anymore."

Kessa knelt down and looked at Arthur, who simply patted Lola's neck. Just as with Bucky, Mihku, and Sippy, Kessa had received the communication in her mind, as if the words had been poured right into her head.

"We need to get her back into the shady area over here under the deck and cool her off." Kessa spotted a spigot in the corner where the pen abutted the house beneath the overhanging deck. She summoned all her strength and pulled herself up over the metal fence, ran over to the spigot, and turned the handle until water flooded into the trough below it. It made a high-pitched hissing sound, and Kessa was worried that Lola would be scared or startled by it, but Lola's ears only perked up. Arthur began whistling and clicking his tongue to try to lure her over to the shaded area beside the trough.

Kessa began scooping the water out with her hands and splashing it onto Lola. Arthur told her to aim for Lola's belly and not her back. If her back got wet, it could trap the heat in. Kessa and Arthur worked quickly to cool her off, and eventually the alpaca was able to lean her head into the trough and drink some water. That was when they heard the car pull into the driveway.

Arthur pushed Kessa toward the fence. He helped hoist her over, and after they'd dropped to the ground, they ran back to the woods. Kessa's eyes were stinging with sweat and tears. She didn't want to leave Lola behind.

"She'll be okay," Arthur said. "We can come back tomorrow and make sure she has enough water."

"How can you say she'll be okay? She almost died from the heat right in front of us!"

"I know." Arthur leaned against a tree and rubbed his eyes. "That old man, he just doesn't know how to take care of her. But I don't know what to do."

"We have to come up with a plan. Let's go back to my house for now."

Arthur nodded. They followed the tree line to the very edge of the yard and then dashed across it to get to the road.

"We're only ten minutes away from the lake," he said. "We just need to follow this road for a bit."

But Kessa barely heard him. Her mind was back at the pen with Lola, the words heat and stress pounding in her ears with each heavy clunk of her boots against the tarmac.

. . .

"Let's go at night—after the old man is asleep!" Kessa said as she looked from Arthur to Mille. They were sitting in the dim wood-paneled room at the front of her house. "We can bring a flashlight and trim her coat ourselves. If she doesn't have all that wool on her, she'll be able to keep cool and survive this summer heat."

"Are you serious?! You know that's trespassing, don't you? We could get in a lot of trouble," Millie said. She took a seat on the couch beside the writing nook. When Arthur and Kessa had returned from their outing, Millie had been waiting for them on the front porch swing in her bathing suit, reading a dog-eared copy of Little Women and sipping from a sweating thermos full of some kind of red juice that stained the area around her mouth.

"But Lola needs us! It's going to be in the nineties tomorrow. Can't you imagine how that will be for her? She could die of heatstroke." Kessa threw a pleading glance at Arthur, who was chewing on his thumbnail, a worried look knitting his brows together.

"Kessa's right, Millie. We need to do this. For Lola."

"Well, what are you going to do?" Millie said. "Just sneak in and cut her fluff off with a pair of scissors? Don't you need a special shaver or something?"

Kessa nodded. "You have a point." She hopped over to the writing nook and opened her computer. It took only a few seconds for her to pull up a video on shearing alpacas.

Arthur and Millie leaned in behind her, and they all watched as a woman next to a tethered alpaca explained how not to get kicked during the shearing process. When the woman grabbed a giant shearing tool, Kessa's heart sank. She realized then that she would never be able to safely cut Lola's fleece. She didn't have the equipment or the skills.

"Yeah, that's not gonna happen," Arthur said flatly as the woman picked up the alpaca's hind leg and began buzzing away.

Kessa closed the video and slid the wheeled office chair out of the nook. "I guess the whole thing is a little more complicated than I had thought."

"Did you see the tool she had? Do you know how to lift up an alpaca leg to get it shaved without being kicked in the face? Because I sure don't!" Millie threw her hands up in the air. "This is way above my pay grade, you guys."

"There's got to be something we can do for her." Kessa took a few spins in the office chair and then stared at the wood floor for a minute to ease the dizziness. Her gaze settled on the old dog-biscuit container that held some of Bucky's chew toys. "Oh, I know! We can bring Lola a treat! We need to at least do something while we figure out a long-term solution."

"I think that's doable," Arthur said, nodding and looking rather relieved. He did a quick search on the computer for safe treats to feed alpacas. "It looks like they can eat apples and bananas. Oh, and vegetables like carrots and romaine lettuce."

"That's great," Kessa said, jumping out of the chair. "I have apples and bananas."

"Perfect," Arthur said. "Let's plan to meet down at the lake around eleven, and then we can all go together. Kessa, you bring the food, and I'll bring the big flashlight. I'll show us the way there."

Kessa was pretty sure her dad would be asleep by then, but even if he wasn't, it would be easy to sneak out through the back deck. But what if her dad woke up for some reason and tried to find her and she wasn't there? He would freak out and probably call the police. Maybe he would think she got abducted. What if he caught her while she was trying to get out? The back door was really old and squeaky like the floorboards. But Kessa liked to think that if she had to explain herself, her dad would understand. After all, he was the one who told her about agency, and how could she write a convincing character with agency if she had no idea what that even felt like—to be brave, to be daring, to take matters into her own hands?

There was no way she wouldn't go through with the plan. Besides, Arthur, Millie, and—most importantly—Lola were counting on her.

Chapter 21: Moxie

The stairs creaked as Kessa made her way down, but she wasn't worried about being caught. Her dad's snoring was louder than any of the squeaky floorboards. She crept out the back door and padded down to the lake, wondering if Mihku was asleep and dreaming somewhere high up in the old maple tree. She could hear the soft croak of frogs and the live-wire sound of buzzing insects in all directions. The water was so still and dark it seemed as if the lake itself were sleeping.

As she approached the dock, she spied something that looked like a lightning bug caught beneath the water. But that wasn't possible, was it? The light began to expand into a small orb of rainbow hues. Kessa set her bag full of Lola treats on the sand and knelt down. She peered at the spot where she had seen the light, but the water went dark again, and all she could make out was her own reflection. She walked to the very edge of the dock and dipped her fingers in and moved them around, as if she could part the depths with her hands, but there was no glow. She was about to rise to her feet when she saw the colorful orb flicker again deeper down, lighting up the weeds and rocky mud of the lake's bottom.

What the heck? She leaned forward on the palms of her hands, gripping the edge of the dock, and let out a small gasp. A large fish with glowing rainbow scales rose into view. The water around the fish shimmered and sparkled with little glittering bubbles.

"My name is Moxie. I'm a rainbow trout."

Kessa understood her perfectly even though the fish's mouth silently opened and closed beneath the water. Kessa's own mouth hung open in awe. She had never witnessed such a beautiful creature in her life.

The trout laughed, and a burst of tiny gold bubbles escaped her mouth. The rainbow tint on her glimmering scales dimmed a bit, and she swished her tail so that even more shining bubbles floated to the surface. "I guess you've never seen a fish this glamorous before. Well, I can't blame you—I am quite the catch! Get it? Get it?" Her tinny laughter echoed through Kessa's mind. "You are the one with the Gift, are you not? All the animals—I mean absolutely everyone around here—is talking about it."

"Yes, well," Kessa stammered, "it's kind of new for me to be able to communicate with nonhuman animals in this way. I kind of wish I wasn't the only one."

"You aren't. There are some boys and girls like you here and there, around the world, but they are indeed rare."

"Do you not usually glow like this? Can I only see you because of my powers?"

"That's right. To everyone else, I probably look like just an average rainbow trout"—she rolled her wide saucerlike eyes—"but you are lucky enough to see me in all my glory."

"Moxie is a pretty name. It means 'tough,' like brave, right?"

"Maybe it means that in your language, but where I'm from—which is here, where the first people lived, hundreds and hundreds of years before you—it means 'dark water.' And I do love dark water. Mmm-hm—feels nice, doesn't it? There's nothing like a night swim."

A bright shaft of light lit up the lake from behind, and Arthur called out to Kessa while waving his flashlight. "What are you doing?"

Moxie's glow went out in a flash, and Kessa could no longer see beneath the water. She sprang to her feet and held her hands in front of her face. "Don't point that thing in my eyes! Agh!"

"Oh, sorry," he said, lowering the light to the ground as Kessa made her way off the dock. "Sorry I'm late too. I was waiting for Millie to fall asleep. She almost didn't. I figured this whole thing would be a lot easier without her tagging along."

"Right." Kessa wiped her damp hands against the front of her shorts. "I guess it's for the best, but she was really excited to come with us tonight. Don't you think she'll be upset she missed this?"

Arthur shrugged, and they started on the dirt path out to the road. When they reached the dead-quiet street, Arthur dimmed the flashlight so it was no longer a bobbing high beam dancing along the berm. "You've got moxie, Kessa."

"What?" Kessa nearly tripped over her own feet. How could he know about Moxie? Had he seen her talking to the fish? The dazzling rainbow glow beneath the water?

"Oh, I just meant you've got guts. I mean, I wasn't sure you would be up for this kind of thing."

Kessa breathed a sigh of relief and shoved him a bit with her right shoulder. "Don't mess with me. I'm telling you, Arthur—I don't always show it but I'm actually kind of a badass." She smirked at the stars, and Arthur leaned into her a bit, but he didn't shove her. He took hold of her hand. Kessa allowed herself to smile wildly, since she knew he wouldn't be able to see her elated expression in the dark, especially with the way her hair made a nice curtain against the side of her face. Everything was just so warm and electric and amazing.

And on top of it all, she had moxie.

・・・

When they arrived at the house, it was clear to them that the old man who lived there was awake. The light from the TV flashed and bounced around the room at the front of the house. They were looking into the window from the other side of the road, their flashlight off.

"How can he still be up!?" Arthur cried. "Don't old people sleep a lot?"

"Well, he's in that front room and probably won't leave if he's watching a show. We can just sneak around back to where Lola is, and he'll never see us. And if we're really quiet, he won't hear us either." She tugged on Arthur's resisting hand, and they crossed the street and ran into the backyard together.

"Now you've got too much moxie. Let's go back. It's too risky with him still being up. I mean, it's one thing to break and enter when nobody's home or if they're sleeping, but when people are home and awake, it's generally a no-go. We'll get caught for sure."

"Who said anything about breaking and entering? All we're doing is dropping off some food for a hungry animal." Kessa marched ahead to where the pen was and asked Arthur to help hoist her over the fence.

"I can't believe we're doing this," he whispered, lacing his hands together to give her a good foothold.

"Oh, we're doing this all right." Kessa chucked her bag to the ground and hopped inside the pen. Arthur jumped in after her.

Lola was awake. When she saw them, she started making a low humming noise, and Arthur knelt down to pet her. Kessa took an apple out of her bag and the small knife she brought with her and began hacking the fruit into small pieces. She held out the apple pieces, and Lola eagerly gobbled them up. The alpaca looked into Kessa's eyes as she chewed, and Kessa could physically feel Lola's ravenous hunger in the pit of her own stomach.

"Thank you. He hardly ever feeds me."

Kessa nodded and pulled a carrot stick out of her bag. "Don't worry, we've got more," she whispered as she stroked the fluff on the side of her long neck, relieved to see that Lola had recovered a bit from the day's heat. Sadly, Kessa knew that it was going to be just as hot tomorrow.

"We better go now," Arthur said, standing up and nearly bumping his head on the low-hanging edge of the deck. "We can always bring her more tomorrow."

"Wait, let me just top off her trough first."

Before Arthur could protest, Kessa turned the handle on the spigot. It made a high-pitched whining sound as the water gushed out. "Oh no!" She had forgotten the noise the tap had made the last time she turned it on. Kessa struggled to twist it back, but her hands were so sweaty it was hard to get a good grip.

"Turn it off! Turn it off!" Arthur pleaded in a strangled whisper.

Kessa turned the handle the wrong way and even more water gushed out, with so much force that it began to spray her. By the time she figured out she needed to turn it in the other direction to close the tap, and the loud squeal began to die down, there was another sound, a much worse sound: the back door sliding open. The light above the door flicked on and shone over them like a spotlight. There was no point in trying to run or hide.

"What in the Sam Hill is goin' on back here? Why are you kids in my alpaca pen? Isn't it a bit late for you all to be runnin' around in the middle of the night? You ain't here to rob me, are yeh?"

Arthur stood with his mouth hanging open and raised his hands up by his ears like he was surrendering for the police. "Sir, we—"

"Close your mouth, son, you look like a dadgum trout." The old man pointed his chin at Kessa where she stood beside the spigot, half-soaked. "And what's your story, li'l lady? He drag you into this?" The old man pointed at Arthur, who slowly lowered his hands to his sides.

"Yeah, he's my friend. I'm really sorry for disturbing you. We just wanted to feed your alpaca and pet her and . . . and bring her some treats." Kessa gave what she thought looked like a reassuring smile and gestured to the apples, bananas, and carrot sticks she had pulled out of the bag and set on the ground.

"Ah," he said. "I see. You like Louise, huh?"

"We call her Lola, sir," Arthur said, straightening his back and sticking his hands in his pockets.

"You can call her a can of beans for all I care." The man was hunched forward as he shuffled over to the railing by the stairs, and in the light, Kessa could see how old and feeble he really was. Looking at his gnarled hand on the banister, she imagined it probably would be pretty difficult to turn that knob on the squeaky water spigot. She thought of how her grandfather, who had arthritis, could barely grasp a doorknob. "I don't know the first thing about them silly-lookin' creatures. My son wanted to start raising alpacas for some cockamamie reason, but he ended moving in with his partner somewhere down in York County, and now he doesn't even answer my calls. He left me up here all alone with this thing"—he pointed a shaky finger at Lola—"and, well, I don't know what to do with 'er."

"We don't know a whole lot about how to care for alpacas, but we do know someone who could," Kessa said, looking over at Arthur. It just occurred to her that Pennacook Pines was the perfect place for Lola. "I have a friend named Ruth. I'm sure she would be happy to take Lo—uise and give her a good home."

"Well, you can have 'er, then!" he replied.

She took her phone out of her bag and asked the old man for his name and number. His name was Willard, and she took down his address as well.

"Do you kids need a ride home or anything?"

Kessa and Arthur looked at each other and shook their heads. "No, definitely not," they said.

"Good! Because the doctor said I shouldn't be drivin' at night. Now get on outta here before your parents start wondering where you're at."

"Yes, sir," Arthur said, giving his forehead a tap with the edge of his hand.

They half walked, half ran all the way back home with wild grins on both of their faces for what they had just done, Kessa praying all the while that her dad would still be sound asleep when she returned. And even though she couldn't wait to be back home, safe and sound, she knew she would have to resist the urge to linger by the dark water for a second sighting of Moxie before heading in. But maybe she didn't have to. Maybe it was enough just to know that Moxie was there.

Chapter 22: A Lit Match

Kessa rose early and went out to check on the garden.

"Well, the dog food is gone again," Kessa said as she bent down to observe a hardy patch of mint with only a few bites missing from the leaves.

"And so is my nut and seed stash! I had them hidden right here under the marigolds. Those filthy thieving rabbits." Mihku shook his paw at the sky, looking a bit like he was swatting at invisible bugs.

"Mihku, there's just one thing I don't understand. If the rabbits don't like dog food—if that's what keeps them away—then why are they always eating it?"

Sippy fluttered down into the garden and hopped around, poking her beak into the plants as if looking for clues. "I don't think this is the work of rabbits."

"No, it most certainly is. Azeban has seen them himself, tearing things up in this very garden!"

Sippy cocked her head. "Oh, Mihku, you sweet summer squirrel. Don't you see? Azeban is playing you. Rabbits don't come out at night to pillage gardens! What else has that lying raccoon told you to do for him, huh?"

"Well, he, uh, he did tell me that if the dog food didn't work, we could try melon rinds, banana, rice, apples, or corn." Mihku's tail fell and his eyes slowly drifted to the ground.

Kessa smacked her open palm against her forehead. "How could we have been so gullible? Mihku, you have to tell Azeban to stay out of our garden!"

Sippy tittered. "That won't work. You need to raccoon-proof this place properly or else he's just going to keep coming back."

"Okay, I guess I'll look online for some ideas later, but right now, I have to get ready to go to the sanctuary. Arthur is coming over soon and I need to change."

"A date with the boy next door?" Sippy let a small ripple of song rise up from her throat. "How utterly darling!"

"It's not—it's not a date," Kessa stammered, face burning like a desert sunset. "We are just going to help out Ruth for a little bit."

"Sounds like a daaaaate," Mihku sang as he pranced around the tomato plant.

"Well, explain this to me, okay, and maybe you can actual be useful for once?" Kessa smiled, though her question was a serious one. "So why is it that when I went on a trip to the sanctuary with Arthur last year, it wasn't a date, but now all of the sudden this year, it is?"

"Uhhh, this is a little out of my wheelhouse, to be honest," Mihku said as he stuck his nose into a fluffy orange marigold.

"The difference, my sweet Kessa, is in the color of your face." Sippy fluttered over and perched on Kessa's knee. "You go run along now and have a nice time on your date."

• • •

Kessa had pulled out nearly every item of clothing she had and could not find anything that seemed right. It would be impossibly impractical to wear a skirt or a dress to the sanctuary, but her usual clothes for working with the animals and helping out in the barn just seemed so plain. Kessa turned sideways in the mirror and tucked the front of a basic blue T-shirt into her jeans . . . and then untucked it.

She frowned at her reflection and removed the shirt, quickly casting it down onto the growing "reject" pile on the floor. The next option was a nicer scoop-necked shirt that had a sunflower print, but it came up too short on her long torso, which was a shame because it had fit perfectly last year.

Arthur was down in the kitchen bantering with her dad about which Beatles album was better, Revolver or Abbey Road. Her dad kept threatening to pull out his records and force Arthur to listen to them to prove his point. It was the same treatment Kessa had been through countless times for as long as she could remember. She had long since decided to just agree with whatever he said; otherwise, she could end up stuck on the couch for ages while her dad hovered and fiddled endlessly with the needle on the record player.

Kessa took a picture of herself in the mirror before taking off the flowery scoop neck and donning a loose-fitting tank top with fringe at the bottom that had a hippy sort of vibe. Snapping another pic of herself in the mirror, she texted the outfit choices to Toria.

"Sunflowers or bohemian?"

Torias text came back immediately—a useless "Lmao."

Why was she being purposefully unhelpful? Didn't Toria know that she needed fashion guidance now more than ever?

Next was a light blue top with ruffled layers and cutouts that exposed her shoulders. It was a little nicer than an average T-shirt, but it was also kind of impractical for a sunny day at the sanctuary. Because of the shoulder cutouts, she'd have to remember to put sunscreen there, or else she might burn. Good enough.

Her dad's voice floated up the stairs, causing Kessa to rush as she picked up her comb and yanked it straight through the tangles. "Come on in here to the living room, Arthur. Let me just show you one thing. Then you'll see what I mean; you'll get it." He was interrupted by the screen door banging shut, and Kessa could hear the familiar scuff of Millie's flip-flops.

She heard Arthur clear above her dad's usual humming as he puttered around his stacks upon stacks of vinyl. "Millie? How did you know I was over here?" Kessa picked up a note of frustration in his voice.

"Where else would you be, brother dear?" she heard Millie say. "It seems like, lately, all I have to do is find Kessa, and voilà, there you are."

Kessa tramped down the stairs and hopped off the last step, nearly tripping over her pile of shoes at the bottom of the stairs. "Dad, please don't bother my friends, okay?"

"Oh, it's no bother at all—I don't mind. Mr. Caliper has great taste in music," Arthur said with a smile. He was wearing a simple yellow T-shirt. He probably hadn't thought twice about what he would wear today.

Do boys ever have to deal with fashion stress?

Her dad beamed and knelt down to flip through his records. "Why, thank you, Arthur!"

"Hey, Kess, didn't you say you had a cool rock that you wanted to show me?" Arthur leaned his head forward and raised his eyebrows at her.

"Oh! Right. Yeah, it's up in my room." Arthur followed Kessa up the stairs, Millie close behind.

"Millie, go back downstairs," Arthur said. "We will be down in a minute. Promise."

"Why? What are you gonna do?" Her eyes narrowed suspiciously, and she crossed her arms. "Are you planning to leave me behind again?"

"We're just going to look at some stuff."

"Well, I wanna see!"

Arthur sighed and stepped aside, still gripping the doorjamb, and Millie took a running jump onto Kessa's bed.

"You follow us everywhere, Mill."

"So?"

Kessa saw the hurt look that flashed across Millie's pale freckled face, and she rushed in with an offer to make gimp lanyards with her later. It seemed to appease her somewhat, but she hung in the doorway sulkily for a few moments before heading back down to where Kessa's dad was likely eagerly waiting with a few records already in the queue.

Kessa and Arthur sat down on the edge of her bed, and Kessa handed him the smooth blobby-looking stone. He turned it over in his hands. "It's really cool that Ruth gave this to you."

He rattled off some facts about rocks and geodes, but as it had been in many of her classroom lessons, Kessa's mind was far from the topic at hand, focusing instead on the stories she cared about. And presently, the story of his face was so interesting that everything else was merely a blur. She nodded periodically to let him know she was listening, which she wasn't really. She had become rather transfixed by, among other things, the darkness and length of his eyelashes, the small indentation above his upper lip, and the faint lines that curved around the sides of his mouth. There were so many wonderful things to consider.

Would he hold her hand in the car? What happened if the butterflies that tickled in her stomach escaped through her mouth all at once?

"Anyway," he said, handing the rock back to her, "I guess we should take Millie home. Didn't your dad say we would leave at eleven?"

Millie sat downstairs beside Bucky, one hand resting on his back and the other digging into a snack-sized bag of potato chips as she sang along to "Norwegian Wood."

"Hey, strawberry head. Ready to go?" Arthur reached into her chip bag and she snatched it away.

"Go where? Where are we going?"

"Back to the house."

"Why?" Millie stood up and brushed the crumbs from her lap.

"Mom needs your help with Daisy. And it's lunchtime. I bet you're starving."

"She doesn't, it's not, and I'm not. I already ate. Just tell me!" She balled her hands up by her sides. "Where are you guys going?"

"Arthur and I are taking a little trip to Pennacook Pines. You can come next time, okay?" Kessa said while ushering her toward the front door.

"Why can't I come this time?"

Arthur and Kessa exchanged looks.

"It's just, there's not enough room," Kessa said. "See, Bucky will sit up front with my dad, and then there's just two seats in the back, so . . ."

Millie looked utterly crestfallen as she shuffled out onto the front porch. "So I can't come? But Bucky can?"

"He's not doing so great lately. He's really old and sick, and we need to keep an eye on him. Next time, Millie, we will go. Just you and me, okay?"

"Next time, later, later, later. Whatever you can do to get me off your back, right? Just like Candice and Dad. Look, I'm not dumb, okay? I can see when I'm not wanted. I can walk myself home." She jumped down the front steps and bolted across the lawn toward her house, red hair streaking like a lit match sailing over the grass.

Chapter 23: Small Details

When they arrived at the sanctuary, her dad let them out of the car and told them he would be returning home because the heat was going to be too much for Bucky.

"He'll enjoy the air-conditioned ride anyway," he shouted out the window as he backed up in the dusty driveway.

Kessa and Arthur marched toward the barn to look for Ruth and ended up finding her in the greenhouse, which had exploded with even more plant life since Kessa had last been there. Kessa and Arthur immediately gave Willard's information to Ruth and told her all about Lola. Ruth seemed very excited about having an alpaca at the sanctuary and said she would start making special arrangements prior to Lola's arrival. She also promised to check up on Lola every day to make sure she had enough food and water until she could come live at the sanctuary.

Arthur marveled at the many rare things Ruth was growing, blurting out the scientific name for certain plants and looking down into various pots and trays of colorful flowers with a mix of wonder and admiration. Kessa kept her hands in front of her and was conscious not to reach out and touch anything too spontaneously. When a hanging a plant's trail of flowers grazed her shoulder, she took some calming breaths and tried to "act natural" before asking Ruth what they could do to help out.

"Not much in here," she said with a laugh, "unless you want to help me take some of these things down to the roadside."

Ruth had a farm stand where she offered up many of her crops for a small price. The flowers were sold at a bigger flower shop a few towns over where she had a deal with the owner. Though Ruth was retired, she never seemed to struggle with money, and she fully owned the large farmhouse on the sanctuary's property.

Ruth loaded up a small wheelbarrow for each of them and sent them off to the farm stand. The stand operated on an honor system, so if anybody wanted to purchase something, they had to look at the chalkboard price list for what they wanted and then leave the money in the metal box. Ruth said that in all her years, nobody had ever stolen a thing, but if they had, it wouldn't bother her a bit; anyone who needed either food or money enough to thieve it deserved to have it.

There was an abundance of strawberries, broccoli, fennel, rhubarb, chives, parsley, turnips, potatoes, and leeks. One of Ruth's favorite vegan meals was potato leek soup, and it seemed it would be a good year for it—the leeks were the biggest Kessa had ever seen.

"Heads up!" Arthur chucked a bundle of leeks at her, but she only caught one. The rest tumbled to the ground just out of her reach.

"Don't throw them!" she yelled. She bent over to pick up the fallen ones.

"Oh, sorry." He came up behind her and grazed her elbow with a cupped hand. "I thought it was a sure catch."

"It's okay," she said, shaking a loose strand of hair from her face. It wasn't a big deal. It was nothing at all, really. But for some reason, the way he touched her so lightly there, on the elbow, caused such a flurry inside her. It was like a sudden wind sweeping up a swirl of snowflakes, and each one could have landed cool and melty upon her hot cheeks, except the flurry remained fully contained, rapidly whirling around her suddenly erratic heart.

He knelt down beside her and transferred the stalks from the ground into her cradled arms. She rose quickly and piled all of them but one on the stand, keeping an especially large leek to strategically block her face. She couldn't let him see that raw part of her burning right on the outside. Her color was too red and too hot, and the feelings were also all toos. Too much, too strong, too soon, too . . . real.

When they returned the wheelbarrows to the greenhouse, Ruth told them to meet her at the back of the barn. On the way there, Kessa and Arthur stopped for a moment to watch the animals in the pasture. Kessa was hoping to get another glimpse of the bull she had seen last time.

The old rescued carriage horses, Rig and Willa, were all the way on the far side of the pasture. Kessa put her foot up on the wooden fence to see if she could spot the bull. She found him standing beneath the old cottonwood tree.

From the corner of her eye, she noticed Arthur observing her profile, then follow her gaze. He leaned forward on the fence and threw his arm out to point at the tree. "That kind of tree can live up to four hundred years, did you know that? I wonder how old that one is. You can tell it's a female tree because the male trees don't produce those fluffy white seeds like that." Arthur went on about the tree, but Kessa's mind was focused on the bull. Images flickered through her mind, images that she couldn't quite grasp. It was like a picture puzzle that was still in pieces. There was a sadness and yearning for touch and connection coming from the bull, and it compelled Kessa to go to him.

"Let's go in and see if we can get a little closer." Kessa hiked up over the fence, deciding not to wait for permission from Ruth, who had yet to make her way up to the barn.

"Shouldn't we ask Ruth first?" Arthur's eyes flashed back toward the barn and he challenged Kessa's with a warning look before hoisting himself over the fence too. "Kessa! We shouldn't be in here with a new animal. We don't know what he's like or what he's been through. It's too risky. What if he runs at us?"

She waved Arthur off and stopped just a few feet away from the bull. He had a handsome rust-colored coat that darkened to a blackish brown around his face and over his nose. She hadn't asked Ruth what his name was, but as she stepped closer, she heard it clearly.

"Jersey."

The name whispered into her mind, and when she raised her eyes to meet his, images cut through her vision like sharp shafts sunlight filtering through the wooden slats of an old barn roof.

She was so hungry, but she couldn't eat. There was something in the way. It was in her nose, and she couldn't get it out—something bright orange and studded with spikes. Her mother kicked at her as she tried to reach what had once provided an abundance of both nutrition and comfort, but she could not get to the milk; her tongue would not fit through the orange ring. Why was her mommy kicking her away?

Boots clomped all around and snippets of conversation filtered through her consciousness, certain phrases cutting through like broken glass: "Time to send them off." The boots moved closer, and there was a painful tugging sensation in her nose as the spiky thing was removed. A sense of relief washed over her. Finally she would be able to get some milk again. But where was her mother? She looked around and saw a line of other calves, a long line that led to the back of a truck. A strained wail echoed around the farm, and as she turned her head to try to figure out where it was coming from, she realized it was the sound of her mother bellowing in pain. And not just her mother, but others' as well. The tortured chorus only grew louder as, one by one, her young brothers and cousins stepped up the ramp to the trailer, kept in a tight line by the boots. Her mother's cries ripping through everything, tearing her whole world apart as she bolted from the lineup and fled straight for the woods at the edge of the field.

Kessa shook her head and looked up. Stark, bare limbs twisted across the sky, and the ground was covered in white. Long legs circled around her like a protective cage as a svelte creature bent down and gently nudged her side. The poking grew more and more intrusive as she struggled to stand up. "Stop. Stop it!"

"Kessa." The large amber eyes of a deer peered into her own, and in them, she saw her own reflection. She was not a lost calf but a human girl, hair flying in all directions and a wild thumping in her chest. As the deer backed away, she could see the face morphing into that of an old woman. It was Ruth, gripping Kessa by the shoulders, her earnest gaze pleading for Kessa to return to her human senses.

"I saw her fall to the ground, but I couldn't get her to wake up. That's when I ran to get you." Arthur was breathing heavily and talking to Ruth as she propped Kessa up against the cottonwood tree. "Is she all right? Did she pass out or something?" Arthur looked at her, a knot of worry between his brows.

"She'll be fine. It's probably this heat—it's been quite intense, and I doubt she's had anything to drink in a while. Arthur, would you please go back to the greenhouse and fill up a fresh water bottle for Kessa?"

As Arthur sprinted away, Kessa looked nervously into Ruth's trusting eyes as the familiar woozy and disoriented feeling slowly began to fade away. "I think it happened again," she said, then swallowed, her throat hot and dry. "Just like before, with the geese."

Ruth nodded. "Much like the geese, Jersey here has been through a lot of trauma." She tilted her head toward the rust-colored cow standing beside them, his dark eyelashes blinked away a few hovering flies.

Ruth explained that Jersey, at only five months old, had been on the way to an auction where he and many other calves were to be sold for slaughter. He made his daring escape while waiting in line to get on the truck and survived by hiding out in the forest, until a few weeks later when he was spotted at the edge of someone's yard where it abutted the woods. Thankfully the couple who spotted him were animal advocates and called Pennacook Pines to see if Ruth could take him.

Kessa drew in a deep breath and got to her feet. She looked into the young bull's eyes, and then her gaze drifted to his nose. "Did Jersey ever have to wear a spiky ring in his nose?"

"Yes, it's a calf weaning device. When calves are born on a dairy farm, they are kept away from their mother's milk. The ring in the nose makes it impossible for them to suckle, and the spikes make it too uncomfortable for the mother when the calf tries to go near the udder."

Jersey trotted several yards away from them as Arthur approached with water bottle in hand. "I went as fast as I could. Should we call your dad?"

"No, I'm fine. Ruth was right—it was just the heat that got to me," Kessa said. She took a long cool drink from the bottle and kept an eye on the bull standing alone out under the sun.

"Why don't you two go over to the pond and feed the geese while I make you up some lunch." Ruth reached into her rucksack and handed them a paper bag filled with alfalfa sprouts. "Feel free to snack on those yourself if ya like." She leaned to her side and winced slightly as she got back to her feet. "I've got something for your dog as well, but it's back at the house. Let's meet at the picnic table in a half hour."

. . .

Kessa's eyes flicked over to Arthur's face as they sat on the picnic rock together side by side. She wanted more than ever to take in all the small details once again, while she was close to him. There were things she had missed last time, like the pale scar on his neck, just below his left ear, or the way his jaw slightly changed shape when he clenched his teeth. His eyes were squinting now, as if looking into bright sunlight, but it was all shade beneath the old willow.

Kessa tossed the remaining sprouts from her bag to the geese clustered in the pond below just a few yards away. She dipped her toes into the water. The two of them sat in silence and watched the geese for a few minutes until Arthur spoke up.

"Have you noticed that my dad hasn't been around at all when you've come by?" He broke a long reed in half and chucked it into the water.

"Yeah, but he's usually away. Doesn't he take a lot of trips for work?"

"Not for half a year."

"He's been on a trip for that long? That's terrible!" She glanced at him again, and this time his whole face was twisted up.

"No, Kessa, he left."

"Oh." A strange numbness spread through her chest. Even though she wasn't old enough to remember when her own parents divorced, she knew that it had changed everything about how she might have lived her life. She tried not to think about it too often, but sometimes, in the quietest, darkest nights, as she waited for sleep, she would let herself wonder.

"He left last year. He's been gone for about six months now. He got an apartment somewhere down in Portland. He's asked me to come visit him a bunch of times, but I haven't. I'm not going. I couldn't do that to Mom."

"I'm sorry," she said in a breath of sympathy. "My parents, they're not together. I know it's not the same, though. They separated when I was a baby." She used her right thumbnail to dig out the thin line of dirt caked beneath the left one.

Arthur started up again as if he hadn't heard her at all. "My mom has just been . . . She's been so weird. She never does anything. She says she's out there painting, but all she's doing is drinking and watching her dumb shows on that old TV set. She won't even act like . . ." His voice broke, and a single wet line cut across his flushed cheek. He shook his head and dropped it between his knees. "She doesn't act like our mom anymore. She doesn't care about anything. And Daisy, Daisy is always begging for her, but it's like she wants nothing to do with any of us."

Kessa flicked the top of her foot out of the water. The polish job Toria had done before she left had mostly chipped away everywhere except for her big toenail. She thought about Millie and Daisy at home and wondered what they were up to. Would Daisy have fallen asleep somewhere on the floor or the couch by now? Was Millie eating snacks by herself, alone in her blanket fort, or reading something from her leaning tower of books?

Dropping her left hand down into the rocky crevice at her side, she closed her fingers around a small stone that was suspended there. Sometimes it was nice to have something to hold.

"It will be all right," she said softly, not because she believed it, but because it seemed like the kind of thing people were supposed to say in moments like this.

Like a movie she wanted to see but couldn't play a part in, Kessa imaged her right hand reaching out to touch the sleeve of his yellow T-shirt. She thought about what it would feel like if she linked her arm around his and leaned her head against his shoulder, but her hand lay still, unmoving against the bare rock. She studied the rise and fall of Arthur's back. She couldn't see his face, which was shielded by his bent knee, but she could hear him breathing raggedly. The unmistakable sound of sobs being stifled punctuated the silence hanging between them.

The geese floated around effortlessly as if nothing terrible had ever happened in the world. They were lucky to have survived and to have each other. Jersey was lucky to have survived too, but he was never going to see his mom again. He didn't have anyone. Kessa clenched the stone in her fist one last time and then tossed it out into the pond, watching the surface break with a satisfying plunking sound. The geese startled for a moment but quickly went back to their placid gliding. Arthur's shoulders trembled like the ripples on the water. Escaped gasps and sighs merged with the breeze, all the messy sounds swept away by the merciful hanging branches of the willow.

Part Three

Chapter 24: The Most Beautiful Sound

Suddenly gulping for air, Kessa awoke with a feeling of dread pressing against her chest. Her gaze moved across the ceiling and then to the alarm clock. Her heart was slamming away at an unreasonable speed for 3:19 in the morning. When she turned to look at the black void that was her open door, a surge of panic coursed through her. Kessa brought the blankets up beneath her chin, the nightmare she'd been having floating back into her mind in bits and pieces.

When she was little, she might have gone to her dad's room to wake him up and ask if she could stay in his bed for the rest of the night, but that wasn't an option now, and neither was holding onto Chuck Chuck, the beloved stuffed animal she'd left behind this year. She wished more than anything for the familiar comfort of Chuck Chuck's sweet and raggedy fur. Just thinking about it caused her to relax a bit, and her sleepiness soon overpowered the panic.

As soon as her lids closed, she saw her toes digging into wet sand, the lake gently lapping at her knees. Tall reeds stood all around her like tufted wands reaching up into the sky, and they made her feel small as she looked up at them wavering in the sunlight.

The water was at her chest now, and she gripped the bedsheets for safety, but they passed like liquid through her fingers. Her heart thrashed like a caged animal when she realized there was nothing to stand on anymore, as if the sand had simply melted away beneath her feet. She reached out to grasp on to something, anything, but cool water began to close around her neck, threatening to swallow her whole. She didn't even have time to yell for help, for her nose was already under.

. . .

"I watched a show once about a woman who got a severe injury when a potato exploded in her face. She hadn't poked any holes in it before putting it into the oven." Arthur reached inside the stove to test poke one of the baked potatoes they had put in an hour ago. "When she opened the oven to check on the potatoes, that's when it happened—bam! That's why you have to always remember to fork 'em up a bit before you cook them."

Arthur's voice had changed recently. It was funny the way it would crack and change pitch sometimes. She liked the sound. Thinking about it made a small flush of heat spread across her face, and she hoped any visible redness could be blamed on the warmth coming from the open oven.

"It's too hot for baked potatoes," Millie whined.

"It's all there is until Mom comes back from the store. If you don't like it, just make cereal or something," Arthur said as he stabbed another potato and transferred it to the plate on the counter. "But I think when Kessa is over here, we should eat vegan stuff."

"Thanks. You guys don't have to—it's your house. But I'm happy to share my butter. It's really yummy, and you won't even notice much of a difference." Kessa licked her lips. When they had decided to make the potatoes, she had run over to her house to get the vegan buttery spread from the fridge. She loved potatoes—baked, mashed, or fried—and did not care how hot or cold it was outside, because she would gladly eat them in any weather.

"How would you know it doesn't taste different if you've never had real butter before, huh?" Millie stood with her hands on her hips. She had gathered her fluffy rust-colored bangs and tied them up to get them out of her face. It looked as if she had a big orange sprout bursting from her head.

Kessa just blinked and, without answering, turned back toward Arthur. She knew it was best to just leave Millie be when she was in a feisty mood. "I'll get the plates."

Daisy, wearing a pair of old swim goggles around her neck, toddled around the corner. Her cheeks were puffed up like a chipmunk with a stash of acorns. She waddled side to side, duck-like, and stopped in front of Kessa before spitting five or six small LEGO pieces out of her mouth.

"Oh! Daisy, you can't do that." Kessa tilted Daisy's chin and peered into her small mouth to look for evidence of any more chokables.

"She does that all the time," Millie said as she hoisted herself up onto one of the kitchen counter stools and folded her arms.

"Well, that's really bad. She could choke. She could die if one of those pieces got caught in her throat."

"No, she wouldn't. I know the Heimlich maneuver and I would never let my baby sister die."

Daisy reached for the first metal rung of the stool and tried to climb it but slipped and fell back onto her bottom. Her bloated diaper cushioned the fall. Using her chubby fingers, she picked up the saliva-covered LEGO bricks that she had just spit out onto the floor and set them in a row at the base of the stool. She then looked up at her big sister proudly, waiting for praise.

"Daisy has such pretty eyes. Not like your eyes, Kessa— your eyes are like pond water. Like muddy mud ponds filled with algae," Millie taunted. "Don't you think so Arthur?"

"Hey!" Kessa put a baked potato down in front of Millie and cut it in half. "What is your problem?"

"Mon Dieu! I don't want your stupid vegan butter and you guys are annoying me. I'm going to go up to my blanket fort and read." Millie hopped off the stool and walked out of the room in a huff.

"She's in a mood," Kessa said as she took Millie's stool. Arthur sat down beside her. His shoulder, clad in a faded blue T-shirt that he had worn countless times, brushed up against hers, and the fresh smell of cedar and laundry detergent hit her senses like an electric current.

It was just a T-shirt. It was just Arthur. Just the same old silly, muddy boy who had once pushed her off the dock and laughed at her frustrated screams when she hit the water backside first. The same boy who brought her popsicles when she got so sick one summer with a stomach bug that she couldn't even take a sip of water without throwing up. This was the boy who chased her with flaming marshmallows on the end of long sticks and who buried treasure for her to find in the woods with handmade maps.

So if it was just Arthur, then why did everything feel so different? Kessa reached for the cracked ceramic bowl of sea salt on the table and sprinkled some on her potato, breathing mindfully to slow the rapid hammering in her chest.

"Yeah, she just gets like that sometimes, and it's only been getting worse lately. Don't pay any attention to her. I think your eyes are nice. They're unique. Not only one solid color, you know?" He studied her eyes for a moment. "And there's those little gold starbursts around the pupils."

Her ears went hot. "Thanks. I think it's called hazel." She shifted on her stool and took a bite of her perfectly cooked, perfectly forked-up potato as Daisy bolted down the hall, waving her arms and making kissy faces and singing "Dizzy a fishy, Dizzy a fishy, fishy go bye."

After they ate, Kessa began mashing up a potato for Daisy while Arthur added their plates to the ever-growing pile in the sink. She thought it would be easier for Daisy to eat something soft and mushy since she didn't quite have all her teeth yet. And besides, Kessa was still feeling somewhat alarmed by the LEGO incident. Mashed potatoes seemed like the least risky food for the already very risk-prone toddler. After adding some salt and a bit of the vegan butter, Kessa poured some juice into a plastic sippy cup and set it on the dirty tray in front of the high chair. The chair was covered in all kinds of sticky food bits, congealed glop, and layers upon layers of old, encrusted crud.

"Does Daisy still eat in this chair?" Kessa asked, her lip curled back in disgust.

"She usually eats on the couch or on the floor in the living room," Arthur said as he filled a cup with water from the faucet.

Kessa went out into the hall and called for Daisy, but she wasn't in the living room, so she padded upstairs to ask Millie.

"She didn't come up here," Millie said, glancing up from her book. "I don't know where she is."

Kessa thumped back down the stairs and met Arthur in the hallway.

"She's not up there?" he asked, eyes registering a shade of panic.

They both dashed for the front door, but it was still firmly latched. The sound of a lamp crashing to the floor startled them, and when Kessa turned around, she caught Sippy taking frantic laps around the room. It was only seconds before she swooped back out through the open window like a torpedo headed for the sky.

The window.

A small stack of cushions from the couch were pushed against the screen-less opening. The parted curtains billowed out with a silent breeze, and Kessa and Arthur exchanged looks for a split second before hurriedly crawling through, one after the other.

Arthur's eyes darted toward the lake. "She's not at the dock. She's probably gone over to my fort—she's always wanting to go in there." Arthur ran to the side of the backyard, but Kessa was pushed in another direction.

She shielded her searching gaze with her hand and flew down the sloping green toward the swampy edge of the lake until her eyes landed on a sandy inlet where the reeds grew extra tall and clustered around the bank. It was there that she caught a flash of what looked like a vertical rainbow beaming up from among the rushes. If she had blinked, she would have missed it, but she knew without a doubt that she had to go right to that spot.

"Daisy!" She let out a scream that pierced the clouds as she tore through the reeds, scanning every inch of the murky surface before catching a glimpse of Moxie's shimmering tail flicking side to side and creating a trail of golden bubbles. She followed the trail, slicing through rushes, and with the cattails tapping at her back, she emerged into clearer water.

Just beneath the surface of the lake, Daisy's fear-struck eyes were wide open, her tiny hands clawing for the surface, opening and closing like two frantic upside-down jellyfish. The lake crept up around Kessa's thighs as she lunged forward and thrust her arms around Daisy's helpless form as it thrashed around.

Arthur was there, ready and waiting as she lay Daisy on the shore. He initiated CPR immediately, tilting her head back to open her airway and listening for a moment to see if she was breathing. Then, bracing his hands on the ground, he pushed his breath into her parted mouth and gave a round of compressions to her chest. As he leaned forward once more for another two breaths, Millie, followed by Candice with a tote of groceries slung over her shoulder, came stumbling down the hill, and Daisy let out a series of strangled, choking coughs that gave way to uncontrollable sobbing. Her pale face reddened as Kessa gathered the traumatized toddler in her arms, Daisy's small body heaving and spasming with each terrified wail.

The Most Beautiful Sound

It was, without a doubt, the most beautiful sound she had ever heard.

Chapter 25: Channel 5 News

After the incident, Kessa had raced over to her house to tell her dad everything that had happened, before heading back to Arthur and Millie's a few hours later to check on Daisy. Millie unlatched the door for her, and as Kessa walked into the living room, Candice met her with a giant hug and an invitation to stay for dinner.

"You better stay," Millie said. "Candice never cooks, so this is, like, a once-in-a-lifetime event, not to be missed." She rolled her eyes and walked over to the couch.

Candice took a spot on the floor and ran her fingers through Daisy's sparse curls. Daisy was sticking her tongue out and smooshing a giant ball of Play-Doh between her marker-covered palms.

"Kessa, I just can't thank you enough." Candice looked up at her, her faded blue eyes blinking back tears. "I hate to think what would have happened if . . ." She swallowed and looked down at Daisy, shaking her head silently as big wet drops fell from her eyes and dotted Daisy's arms.

Daisy pointed her finger at the stairs and declared, "Otter here." Everyone looked toward the hallway.

Arthur stopped on the bottom stair near the giant box of diapers and dropped his head. "It was my fault. I should have been watching her better."

"We all should have," Millie said, drawing her legs into a folded position on the sofa. "If I hadn't gone up to my room and left those cushions beside the window, this probably never would have happened."

Candice drew Daisy into her lap and hugged her close. "You kids are all I've got. I'm not ever going to leave you alone again."

"I just can't believe you actually saved her. How did you know she had gone down to the rushy area? It's impossible to even see the lake there through all those reeds and cattails." Millie stared at Kessa and bounced on the seat cushion. "Maybe you'll become famous now. You'll be a local hero." She paused and bit her fingernail for a moment. "No. Heroine. You are a heroine, Kessa. Hey, we should call the news and tell them. Maybe you'll get an award!"

"Kessa is indeed a heroine," Candice said, "and she was very brave, and we are incredibly thankful, but we are not going to discuss our private matters with the media."

"Well, then maybe this is a job for Channel 5. Right, Arthur?" Millie jumped up and picked through a small basket of toys beside the stone hearth until she pulled out a large wooden spoon, which was partially blackened with soot from where Daisy had obviously used it to investigate the fireplace. Millie straightened her back and held the spoon firmly in front of her chin.

Arthur put his hand on the back of his neck and flashed a crooked smile at Kessa. "We used to do this when we were little. We just had this thing where we made up news stories."

"Hey!" Millie said. "This is the first real story that our channel has ever reported on. No way am I going to miss this opportunity."

Daisy clapped her hands and reached for the Play-Doh that rolled off her lap. Candice chuckled and used her delicate fingers to wipe away the tears clinging to her lower lashes. "You two haven't done that old routine in ages."

Millie turned to the wall and fixed her gaze on an invisible camera. "Hello, this is Millicent the Magnificent, reporting for Channel 5 News about the daring rescue of a toddler who was pulled from Lake Wabanaki earlier today." Millie paused to wave Arthur over with an impatient hand gesture. "And I have with me my assistant, outdoor survival enthusiast and Wabanaki Lake resident Arthur the Amazing. Over to you, Arthur." Millie nodded seriously and handed the wooden spoon to Arthur, who smiled broadly.

"Ah, yes, thank you, Millicent. Today we are interviewing Kessa Caliper, who heroically saved the life of a young child just this afternoon." He thrust the wooden spoon at her. "Tell us more about your heroic deed, Miss Caliper."

"I'm not a hero. I just did what anyone would do," she said with a shrug. "I'm glad little Daisy is okay. I would do anything to help save a life—anything."

Arthur was beaming at her like she'd never seen before, his lit-up eyes a bright spotlight just for her. "And Miss Caliper, I hear you are vegan, which means you probably save countless animal lives as well, simply by not eating them."

She didn't even try to hold it back—the smile spread across her face like a time-lapse flower blooming. "Yup! I'm just an average vegan teen."

"Well, I think it's safe to say that there is absolutely nothing average about you, Kessa Caliper. Back to you, Millicent."

"Channel 5 has also heard that Kessa has made strides to help save a neglected alpaca on Route 1 who was in desperate need of help. Do you have any updates for us, Arthur?"

"Yes, thanks to Kessa and her unending bravery, Lola is being taken in by Pennacook Pines Animal Sanctuary and will be well cared for by the kind owner who lives there. Ruth has lots of experience with all kinds of animals from various backgrounds."

"Oh yeah," Kessa said, breaking the news routine. "I meant to ask you why you named her Lola."

"I would rather not say," Arthur said. He tossed the wooden spoon onto the couch.

"I know why!" Millie screeched.

Arthur shot her a warning look and then rolled his eyes.

"I'm gonna tell her," Millie said, hopping from foot to foot with excitement.

"No, I'll tell her. I don't care. It's really not a big deal," Arthur muttered as he avoided making eye contact with Kessa, who was growing more curious by the second.

"I, uhh," Arthur stammered, "I used to have a llama Beanie Baby named Lola. It was on her tag. Our alpaca Lola looks just like her . . . well, except for the multicolor patches." He took a small bow and threw his arm out to the side in a sweeping motion while keeping his head low, but Kessa could see he was blushing a bit. "So now you know."

"You had a Beanie Baby?" Kessa bit the edge of her tongue, but she couldn't stop her smile.

"Beanie Babies, actually. One might even have called it a . . ." Millie paused and cocked her head to the side. ". . . collection." She rocked back and forth on her heels, a very self-satisfied grin plastered across her face.

"Whatever, Mill! You had them too." He gave her shoulder a playful shove, and Millie stuck her tongue out at him.

Arthur looked at Kessa and crossed his arms. He almost looked a bit proud now, the magenta remnants of embarrassment fading from his cheeks. "Lola wasn't a 2.0, but I had almost everyone from the 2.0 line—even Shearsly the Lamb and Quackly the Duck. The whole line was discontinued after only a year in 2009. Go ahead and make fun of me if you want, but when I sold them all on eBay, I was able to buy a really cool moun-tain bike."

"A used one," Millie scoffed.

"That's kind of cool, though," Kessa said. "Do you still have it?"

"Nah. I couldn't fix it, so I just took it apart."

"Well, none of that matters anyway," Kessa said, raising her chin and trying to suppress her laughter for Arthur's sake. "The important thing is that the real Lola is safe with Ruth now. Ruth told me she was contacted by someone a few towns west who can't handle their alpacas anymore, and she'll be taking them in. So Lola will finally have some friends!"

Millie clapped her hands together. "This is the best news day Channel 5 has ever had! Now," she said, turning to address her mom, who was on the floor trying to keep Daisy from eating the Play-Doh, "what's for dinner?"

Chapter 26: The Whole Shebang

Kessa wrinkled her nose in disgust as she searched online for natural ways to protect the garden. Coyote urine? Blood meal? There was no way she was going to use either of those on her plants. She sat on the edge of her bed and scrolled through a few more articles, each less helpful than the last.

She mumbled to herself as she rose to take another look in the mirror. "Azeban can just keep snacking. I'll use my hands to regrow everything if I have to. Sneaky raccoon! I wish Mihku could tell him to stay away." She ran a comb through her hair, but the humidity in the air had created a permanent halo of frizz around her head.

As she reached her hands up to smooth the top of her crown, the doorbell rang, and her heart picked up a new pace. She had been anticipating this dance at the community center in town ever since Arthur had mentioned it a few weeks ago on the night of her birthday. At first, it had only seemed like another fun thing to do to punctuate the endless summer weeks, but now . . . now it had somehow turned into an event that transformed her gut into a blender at the mere thought of it. Why couldn't her hair just stay flat and sleek?

Kessa hopped down the stairs and rounded the corner. Arthur was in the hallway near the kitchen, and she stood before him for a moment with her mouth agape. He was wearing pants she'd never seen him in before, the kind with a long crease running down the front of each leg. He had on a white collared dress shirt with the sleeves rolled up high on his forearms, the cuffs hanging out. She could tell he had tried to tame his dark fluffy bangs, but they were already falling out of place.

She wanted to say something like "What is this? School picture day?" That was what Toria liked to say to boys if they were looking too dressed up or their hair was shiny with gel. But then he smiled at her with that broad elastic grin, and any witty comment that might have had a chance to escape simply melted away and slid back down her throat like warm ice cream. It wouldn't have made sense anyway. He doesn't go to school.

She climbed into the back seat of their old 2001 Range Rover and fastened her belt buckle. She smiled at Millie and Millie briefly smiled back, but then her expression almost as quickly changed to a glower. Saving her little sister from drowning apparently hadn't improved her attitude toward Kessa all that much.

"You'd better watch out, Miss Kessa," Millie taunted. "You're gonna have a lot of competition. All the ladies always want to dance with Arthur." She smirked and pulled the ginger frizz of her bangs into a sloppy sprout with one of the many colored elastics that lined her wrists.

Kessa swallowed, a rising panic pushing back against the inside of her ribs. She had been so happy that he had asked her to come to the dance that she hadn't really thought that there might be other girls there who would want to dance with him too.

Sitting beside Daisy, who sat in the middle in her rear-facing bucket seat, Kessa felt her forehead grow slick with sweat as she waited for Candice to turn on the air-conditioning. Up in the front passenger seat, Arthur tuned the radio, and the music got Daisy kicking her sandaled feet. She leaned forward to look at Kessa with a sweet smile that clearly hadn't been wiped after her last meal. Kessa reached into the car seat and tugged playfully at Daisy's little toes, which sent her into a fit of cherubic giggles.

"I know it's a tad warm in here," Candice shouted as she rolled down the side windows, "but this car hasn't had air-conditioning since 2010!" She laughed like it was a wonderful thing to be driving in a hot car on a humid day. Her faded auburn hair caught the wind, and stray strands became entangled with the long beaded earrings that grazed her shoulders.

Arthur turned around in his seat to look at Kessa. "What kind of music do you want?" he shouted, his voice competing with the rushing air from the open windows on an all sides.

"Beatles!" she shot back reflexively. "Beatles or, you know"—she lowered her voice a bit—"whatever. It doesn't matter. I like pretty much anything."

"You're just saying the Beatles because you know we like the Beatles," Millie hissed. "Arthur and I always listen to the Beatles. We liked them first."

"Um, I'll have you know, Millipede, that I have been listening to the Beatles since before you were born. My dad has made sure of that."

Millie crossed her arms and glared at that seat back in front of her as Arthur flipped through an old CD case and slid Rubber Soul into the slot on the dash.

As they got closer to the center of town, Kessa pulled out her phone to check the signal and shot Maddy and Toria a text. "About to go to the dance with Arthur! Wish me luck! Hope I don't fall on my face lol."

As Candice parked the car, Kessa wiped her damp palms over the light pink fabric covering her thighs. It was a good thing Toria had suggested a skirt with spandex workout shorts underneath, in case Arthur was going to try any of those flipping moves on her like he had with Millie. The last thing she wanted to do was show off her underwear to a room full of strangers.

When they walked through the massive wooden doors of the community center, Kessa could hardly believe her eyes. Aside from one younger couple who were wearing all black and practicing in the corner, the rest of the crowd was made up of people her parents age and quite a few who looked like they were probably grandmothers and grandfathers.

Candice strode over to talk to a middle-aged balding man sitting in one of the many chairs lined up against the wall. The man greeted her with a wide smile as she took a seat next to him, plopped Daisy down beside her, and passed her phone into the toddler's outstretched hands.

"Is this senior night or something?" she whispered as Arthur approached a group of old ladies who were beckoning to him. Millie snickered, seeming fully satisfied with Kessa's look of surprise, and skipped ahead to take her place by Arthur's side. Arthur flashed Kessa a smile and waved her over.

"Helen, Lottie, Pearl, I'd like you to meet Kessa. She lives next door to me in the summer."

"Arthur, she's lovely, just lovely," Helen said. Her long gray hair was twisted into a bun at the nape of her neck, and she nodded at Kessa with kind eyes.

Lottie, whose hair was short and a glossy jet black with smooth waves, clasped her hands in front of her and looked from Kessa to Arthur with a large grin that displayed her yellow-tinged enamel. "What an absolute doll she is."

"Yes," added Pearl, who looked like she had recently raided a costume shop for beaded jewelry, "but now it's more competition for us."

The ladies tittered and Helen flapped her hand out in front of her. "Oh, Pearl!"

"Nice to meet you all." Kessa, still in shock, swept her eyes around the room one more time, then turned back to the ladies.

She tried to imagine Arthur doing a swing dance flip with one of them, and a bemused look fell across her face. "So, you're all here to dance?"

Helen pointed to an old man seated in the corner. He was reading a book and looked completely absorbed by the pages, unaffected by the music coming from the speakers all around the room. "That's my husband, Sherman. He drove us here. He doesn't dance." She rolled her eyes and gave an exaggerated sigh.

"My husband doesn't dance either. Well, he would like to, but he can't. He's got a bad back." Pearl gave a sympathetic nod.

"And my husband is dead!" Lottie titled her head back and let out a loud cackle that bounced up to the ceiling. The other ladies chuckled, clearly well accustomed to her particular sense of humor.

"You ladies are such a hoot!" said Arthur. "Are we starting with swing tonight, foxtrot, or waltz?" The couple in black had moved to the small stage at the front of the room and were hooking a microphone into a stand. "Looks like Needra and Quin are about ready!"

Arthur explained that the couple onstage were experienced ballroom dancers who had moved to the area last year, and began offering free lessons at the community center. Though they were not as old as the rest of the crowd, it seemed as though Kessa would not be meeting any new friends her own age. On the other hand, she did feel relieved she wouldn't have the kind "competition" that Millie had hinted at in the car.

• • •

After a few warm-up waltzes, where Arthur took turns with Kessa and the older ladies, the swing music came on. Millie hopped out of her seat and trotted out onto the floor.

"C'mon, Arthur!" she said, tugging on his arm.

"I haven't really had that much of a chance to dance with Kessa, and you already know how to swing. Go sit with Mom and Daisy for a while or just dance on your own for now, okay? Please?" He tilted his head and raised a brow at her.

"I don't want to. I'm bored. Mom is talking to the bald guy again, and Daisy won't let me have the phone." Millie huffed but marched across the room and went back to her book.

Kessa was beginning to get the hang of the steps, and Needra, the instructor, came over to give her some pointers. Needra's hair was slicked back into a high bun, and she smelled of flowers, vanilla, and something like freshly baked cinnamon buns.

"You're doing a great job leading, Arthur," she said, "but why don't you let me help your friend for a moment here." When she stepped in and took Kessa's hands, it was as if gliding across the floor was a natural movement for Kessa's untrained feet. "I'm leading for you right now so you can get the feel of it. Just listen to the music and make sure you're on the count. Quick, quick, slow. Quick, quick, slow." Before Kessa knew what was happening, Needra spun her around, and she somehow landed right back where she was supposed to without missing a beat.

Kessa let out a bright burst of laughter. "This is really fun!" she shouted over the music.

Needra, her head held high, smiled with her broad chin lifted. "Come back in two weeks," she said in a thick German accent. "I'll teach you some more." She winked.

. . .

Toward the end of the night, Kessa spotted Arthur in the corner of the room beside the stage helping himself to a drink at the water cooler. She followed the path of his gaze as he glowered at his mom and the bald man she was talking to. Millie was on the floor beside Daisy, who squatted comfortably while watching something on Candice's phone, her face reflecting a bluish glow as Millie's finger flicked around the screen.

Kessa headed over to Arthur.

"Did you see me out there?" she said. "Needra is amazing. She just pulled me out onto the floor again, and it was like she was controlling me somehow. She made me dance good, and I'm not good!"

Arthur's eyes flicked over to her briefly as if her words were a distraction before homing in again on where his mom sat. Candice was gesturing wildly with her hands in the way people tend to do when they are engrossed in telling a story.

"See that guy over there?" Arthur raised his hand with the cup in it, and some water splashed out.

"The bald guy?" The man touched Candice's arm as his face registered delight in whatever she was telling him, but Kessa couldn't make out anything they were saying all the way across the room. "Do they know each other?"

Arthur took another drink and tossed the paper cup into the trash. His cheeks were flushed, lips even redder than usual. "He's hitting on her."

"Maybe she just wants to make some friends?"

Arthur shook his head, the glare fading from his eyes. "It doesn't matter, I guess. I'm just glad you came with us." He craned his head around to survey the room. Some of the crowd was already filtering out into the night, especially the elderly ones. Helen and Pearl disappeared through the door, followed by Lottie, her dark hair slightly askew.

"The triplets are leaving. Now I'll have you all to myself." Arthur grinned and pulled Kessa by the hand back out onto the dance floor.

Needra's dance partner, Quin, who sported a delicate and precise goatee, leaned into the microphone and announced that the night was wrapping up, but anyone who wanted to practice some intermediate moves could stay for more individual instruction. He waved at Millie, who had joined them at the front of the room.

The dance instructors approached the three of them to demonstrate a few different flips. First, Quin flipped Needra over his arm, and then they showed them something called the cradle swap.

"Arthur, you already know these," Quin said, "so why don't you practice with your friend here"—he nodded at Kessa—"and Needra will stand by to spot you." He looked at Millie and smiled kindly. "And I'll take the redhead!"

"What?" Millie shouted. "Why can't Kessa go with Quin?"

Needra's voice was as measured and elegant as her posture. "I'm going to assist Arthur and Kessa with some basic lifts, and this will give you a chance to do some more advanced moves with Quin."

Millie stamped her foot. "But me and Arth—" She took a deep breath. "Arthur and I usually practice the flips together."

Kessa held out a conciliatory hand. "C'mon, Mill, we're just having fun—all of us together."

"No! You"—Millie thrust a fierce pointer finger at Kessa—" have ruined everything. It's like you don't even want to play with me at all anymore. Every summer, it used to be way more you and me, and now it's just you guys hanging out together and pushing me away constantly." She choked on the word as a sob forced its way out of her throat and tears began to well up behind her pale lashes. "He's my brother and he would rather hang out with you. All you guys wanna do is your own stuff together without me. You even left me out of the Lola adventure. The Lola adventure! That was supposed to be all of us! Well, I've had enough of this whole shebang! Nobody wants me—not you, not Candice, not Dad. Nobody!"

Millie looked down at the floor, swiped at her wet cheeks, and then raised her eyes to glare at Kessa once more. "He built a whole fort for you just to watch the fireworks. Do you even care?" She hiccupped through her tears and walked out of the hall, shoulders shaking, the sound of her plastic flip-flops slapping across the floor. Arthur met Kessa's eyes for a moment and opened his mouth as if to say something but then returned his gaze to his shoes, his posture slack as a pair of old jeans.

She felt like she should do something, but she didn't know what. "Should I go after her?"

Arthur folded his arms across his chest and studied Kessa's face for a few seconds before looking back at the massive wooden doors that stood open to the night. "Nah. I'll go talk to her."

Needra and Quin gave Kessa a sympathetic nod and began packing up their stuff. Kessa let a few minutes go by before she poked her head outside. Scanning the parking lot, she made out a hunched shadow beneath the streetlight and ran across the tarmac to find Arthur sitting on the curb, picking apart a long blade of grass.

"Hey. Where is she?"

"She's sitting in the car. She won't come out."

He lifted his chin in the direction of the car. Kessa could hardly make it out, but a dark figure was moving around in the back seat of the old Range Rover parked in the far corner of the lot.

"We'll just have to wait for my mom." He looked at his watch. "I can't believe she's been talking to that dude all night. She probably doesn't even realize the dance is over." A sound of disgust came from somewhere deep in his throat.

The still humid heat of the evening threatened to steal the air from Kessa's lungs, so she just held her breath, biting down on the back of her tongue. For a few moments, she fixed her eyes on the streetlight and listened to the rhythmic chorus of crickets rise and fall with the clicking sounds of katydids in the tall grass.

"Was that true, what Millie said? Did you really build that fort for me?"

Arthur winced and propped one elbow on his bent knee, pressing a palm to his forehead. As he leaned forward, his shaggy bangs fell over the back of his hand. He said nothing.

"Well . . . whether you did or not, I just want you to know, it was pretty much the coolest thing I've ever seen."

"Kessa." He closed his mouth and let out a puff of air from his nose. "Look, I'll just tell you, all right? I've liked you—I mean, I've had this thing for you for I don't even know how long." He let out a strangled sigh, and his voice cracked as he struggled to get the words out. "You must think I'm such an idiot."

"No. No, I don't think that at all. I just didn't have any idea. Not until the fireworks, anyway . . ." She trailed off. "Then I kind of wondered." Why couldn't she just say it? It was only four simple words—I like you too—sticking to the roof of her mouth like peanut butter. She had a sinking feeling that she wasn't doing this whole crush thing right. Kessa sat down and stared at the tarmac, then ran her fingertips along its warm and bumpy surface. It seemed to have all the heat of the summer soaked right into it.

"So, are we okay, then?" Arthur looked at her with brows raised, dark forest eyes pleading.

"Yeah, we're cool," Kessa said, not knowing what that meant or if it even mattered. There was clearly no going back to the way things were. He wasn't just the same old Arthur; things were different now. And she wasn't exactly the same old her either, but that would just have to be okay for the time being.

Chapter 27: Bucky

Like a glass of water sullied with a single drop of almond milk: that was what the sky looked like, its low clouds indistinguishable from one another as they blended into a vast foggy whiteness tinged with a dismal grayish blue.

Kessa liked how her dad always said the same thing on typical hazy days in August: "If it were any more humid, it would be raining." And everyone hoped it would rain too. It had been unbearably hot the previous week, and now, after many more days, the sky would cloud over and get dark every afternoon, but nothing would happen. The grass was beginning to turn patchy and brown, and the constant heat drove Kessa into the lake at least twice a day.

After working on her story all morning, Kessa pulled on her old one-piece bathing suit with the stripes on the side. She was getting ready to meet Arthur and Millie down at the dock for an afternoon swim. They needed her dad to come back from Bucky's surgery appointment soon, because they weren't allowed to go in the lake without an adult around, and Candice had taken Daisy with her to the store. He had said he would be back by two, but now it was nearly three, and the swampy air just seemed to be getting more oppressive by the minute.

Even though the sun would not be beating down on them directly due to the cloud cover, Kessa made sure to put her sunscreen on, because as her mother had reminded her countless times, it was still possible to get a bad burn even if you couldn't see the sun.

Kessa had learned that the hard way last summer when she spent most of one overcast day sitting out on the dock in her bathing suit reading a chapter book that she couldn't tear herself away from. Sometime after supper, a feverish feeling had hit her, and when she pressed a finger to her skin, it left a pale imprint against the deepening red that spread across her chest and shoulders. She had gone on to spend three painful nights writhing and whimpering in her bed, unable to find a comfortable position that wouldn't irritate her blistering skin.

Several days later, Kessa was molting like a snake, and Millie had carefully peeled sheets of skin from her back. Millie had confessed she was going to keep it in a jar at home that she kept specifically to "put gross stuff in," which Kessa had thought was entirely disgusting, though she herself had delighted in rolling the translucent peelings from her chest between her fingertips into small, spongy white balls.

Fully slathered with an abundance of white streaks and eager to get out to the lake, Kessa bounded out of her room and made it halfway down the stairs when her dad entered the front doorway. She stopped midstep as her eyes darted to the collar in his hand. Bucky's collar.

"How did the surgery go? Where is he?" Kessa peered over her dad's shoulder, expecting to see Bucky lumbering slowly along. "Did they fix his eyes? Can he see now?"

Her dad looked at the collar hanging loosely from his fingertips. With an almost imperceptible shake of his head, he cast his gaze to the floor.

"Dad? Where is Bucky?"

"Kessa." He took a step toward her.

"Dad! Where is he?" The whites of her eyes burned, singeing beneath her lashes.

"Kessa, he's not . . ." He shook his head again. She could see the depth of his breath with the rise and fall of his chest. He had on one of his usual worn T-shirts, so threadbare that the design on the front, whatever it was, had long ago faded. "He's not coming—"

"No! You need to go back there and get him. Right. Now! Dad. Go and get him." She held onto the banister, gripping it until her knuckles went white. "Please!" She choked out a small sob, and everything went blurry.

This was not how she would have written it. This wasn't the way her story was supposed to go. If she could just change this one chapter, everything would be fine. Everything would be okay.

"C'mere." He opened his arms to her. His face was wet, but it was probably just sweat from the heat of the day. She had never seen her dad cry before, so she was certain that was all it was. It had to be.

The blood was rushing hard and fast between her ears. Someone was screaming, some distant voice that sounded like her own, screeching and yelling "GO and GET HIM" over and over. "Go and get him. Go. Just go."

Kessa took off, her bare feet smacking against the hard wooden stairs as she flew through the house toward the back porch. She had to get to the lake. Out of the corner of her eye, she caught Millie and Arthur on the hill as they made their way down to the dock. Within minutes she was standing at the edge of the dock. Her reflection wavered in the water as she took a deep breath before diving in.

She lay back in the water and wrapped her submerged legs around one of the wooden posts that held up the dock. What happens when the air is too hard to breathe? Do you just suffocate or pass out like hikers sometimes do at really high altitudes? If she had gills, she could be free. Where was Moxie? Kessa wanted to go down to the very bottom with her and never come back up.

She pushed herself all the way underwater and opened her eyes to the blurry aquatic landscape and looked upward, the ripples above distorting the sky. Gripping the post, which was slick with algae, she held still and watched as the little bubbles from her nostrils rose to the surface.

No one can tell if you're crying when you're underwater. Mermaids probably never get sad.

Nearly out of air, Kessa held her eyes wide as a pair of feet plunged into her realm and dangled beside her face. She let go of the pole and broke through the surface to see Millie, who had on a mismatched two-piece bathing suit, seated on the dock. Behind her, Arthur was standing in his swimming trunks and looking down at Kessa.

"Wow! You must have been under for at least sixty seconds! Do you want to have a contest? I can do nearly two minutes." He grinned and flung a pair of goggles down onto his towel, which was spread out on the dock.

"Yes!" Millie clapped her hands above her head to get their attention. "I'll do it too! I can hold my breath for a wicked long time, right, Arthur?"

Kessa hoisted herself up onto the dock. The air must have cooled, because the lake was now as warm as a bath, beckoning her to crawl back in. She sat next to Millie and drew her knees into her chest, hugging her legs and looking down at the water.

"Kessa?" Arthur sat beside her and dangled his legs in. He tilted his head to the side and looked at her with care, somehow reading between the rivulets of lake water and the pain.

Little drips fell off her nose and ran down over her mouth. It should have been obvious that they weren't tears because she had just come out of the water and was still drying off, naturally. She had to keep her lips pressed together very tight, or her insides might spill out.

Millie got up and draped her faded mermaid-print towel around Kessa's shoulders.

"You don't have to say anything," Arthur said. "It's okay. Do you want us to go?" Kessa could feel his eyes scanning her face like an X-ray machine.

She sniffled, shook her head, and then buried her nose in her knees. She didn't want to be alone, but she couldn't bring herself to say it. She didn't dare open her mouth. Who knew what would come out if she did? She had to save her tears for the bottom of the lake. Somehow, it was safer that way. That was the story she told herself, and she was sticking to it.

Millie leaned her head against Kessa's shoulder, bits of her wildfire frizz clinging to Kessa's damp arm. Arthur put his hand on her back, and the comforting weight of his palm caused the little salty rivers of water on her cheeks to quicken and pool over her bare kneecaps. They tickled the sides of her legs on the way down to the dock, where they would disappear between the wooden cracks and find their true home in the green waters below. The dripping increased rapidly as the sky finally broke, and the sound of little raindrops pelting the lake and dock rose all around them.

"If there are three people and two of them are happy, the sad one should always be in the middle." Millie edged her right foot over so that her little toe overlapped Kessa's.

"Always."

Chapter 28: Subtle Pressure

The rain had been coming down for days. It just kept coming, and Kessa sat out on the sheltered front porch swing, fully immersed in her required reading for the summer. She had devoured the books quickly and was already on her last one on the list. Since Bucky's death, she had found that reading was one of the few things she could do that truly distracted her from the tearful thoughts that threatened to swallow her up whole if she didn't keep turning the pages.

Normally, she would have taken to writing, but she was stuck on the ending of the story she had started when she arrived and couldn't get passed the writer's block. Why were endings always so difficult?

The garden was doing well; Azeban had not attacked it lately, and the tomato plants were nearly as tall as she was. She would have liked to spend time with Mihku and Sippy, but the frequent torrential downpours kept them away.

During a brief break in the storm when the rain slowed to a drizzle, a series of sloshing sounds caused her to look up from her book. Arthur came around the corner, slogging through the soaked lawn in tall black rain boots. He closed the giant umbrella he was holding and chucked it down beside the stairs before coming up the porch steps.

"Hey, I haven't heard from you in a couple of days. Thought I would come by and see if you were okay."

"Thanks. I've been catching up on my summer reading."

Kessa put her book in her lap and moved over so he would have room to sit on the swing beside her. Without warning, the rain picked up again, causing the water to gush through the gutter and making it a soothing backdrop to the chorus of furious tapping on the roof.

"Have you finished your story yet?"

"Oh." She looked down. Every book she had ever read had an ending. They weren't all great, but at least they were finished, complete works. "No. It's not ready yet. I'm having some issues with some of the supporting characters. But I have to finish it soon because I want to submit it to a contest and the deadline is coming up."

"I wrote a story. I'll read it to you sometime. If you're interested." He ran his fingers along his jaw and paused at the chin, fingertips questioning the texture there. There were no blemishes, no hairs, only perfect, smooth skin. "It's about a tsunami that hits the East Coast. It's actually possible. Nobody thinks it will ever happen, but it could. A flank collapse of La Palma in the Canary Islands is all it would take. It would be catastrophic."

Kessa snorted. "Why do you love disasters so much?"

Arthur just looked at her and blinked. He touched the tip of his tongue to his upper lip and made a funny sound, halfway between a laugh and a sigh. "So, you're going to start middle school pretty soon, right?"

"Speaking of disasters." Kessa pressed her eyes closed for a few seconds, like her mom usually did when presented with questions she didn't want to answer. Aside from Bucky's death, it was the other big thing she didn't want to think about. All those scrambling feelings in her chest that kept her awake at night.

"Yeah, but I don't want to. My best friend, Toria, has been obsessed with starting middle school—I mean, junior high—all year, but she's the kind of girl that junior high will like. She'll fit in. Me on the other hand . . ." She shrugged. "I have no idea if I'll even make new friends. Toria can do it so easily."

"Why are you comparing yourself to some other girl?"

"Don't get me wrong, it's not like I want to be her. I like myself fine. It's just . . ." Kessa twisted her fingers in her lap and took a deep breath. "Her clothes all fit her exactly right, she's got the tan and the makeup, and everything she says comes out slick and snappy, and I'm just—"

"Perfect," Arthur whispered. "You're perfect."

She swallowed and met his eyes. There was a rumble of thunder in the distance, but the lightning was right where she sat, all up and down her spine. His eyes flicked over her face, his intent brows knit together and his cheeks so ruddy it was like he was wearing some of Toria's pink blush. The pit of Kessa's stomach went cold—or was it hot? she couldn't tell—but the sensation was not like anything she had ever felt before.

Then it happened. He leaned forward and pressed his mouth against her lips as if afraid the subtle pressure might break them.

She had never imagined that this was how it would be. Her first kiss, the first kiss of her life—and she had her eyes open. Kessa shut them tight just as Arthur pulled away.

"Are you all right?"

Kessa raised her lids lazily to meet Arthur's concerned gaze as he brought his hands in toward his chest, a forceful thumb pressing into his right palm. The only sound was the blood rushing between her ears. Or was it the rain?

"I've never kissed a girl before. I'm sorry if I—"

"No, it's okay. I just . . . I forgot to close my eyes." She bit her lip to keep her smile in check.

This was no daydream, and even though she had been kissed first, she knew she was in charge of how this story would play out.

So what if things would never be the same between them again? She was no cloud and didn't want to wait any more. Better to be the wind. She liked him. She knew she liked him, and it was okay to let him know. And now, well, now he would know.

"I think . . . we should do that over," she said, the warmth spreading through her chest and rushing to the tips of her fingers.

Arthur laughed. When that smile of his stretched across his face like a rubber band, it made her heart do a backflip all the way up into her throat.

"Okay!" he said, still grinning as he tilted his head.

And then, just like that, there was a second kiss. The second kiss of her life.

. . .

Kessa pounded up the stairs at almost the same rate her heart was beating and shut the bedroom door behind her. She flung herself onto the bed and dug her phone out from the tangle of sheets in the middle, taking shallow breaths as the rain thrashed against the side of the house. She lay back to stare at the ceiling, trying to relive every last moment from out on the porch swing before Arthur had gone home.

It was as easy as pressing rewind in her mind to play again and again how the damp air had made his hair curl out on the sides, how he had put his arm around her after the kiss and the way they sat like that, shoulders touching, until the wind shifted the downpour so it slanted in on them. How in the midst of the driving grayscale hue that encompassed everything, Arthur had turned back to smile at her from beneath the umbrella as he walked toward his house. And the best thing of all was that all of it was hers, hers to reach inside and hold in her mind whenever and wherever she wanted to.

She had hoped to get both of her friends on the phone at the same time, but Maddy hadn't answered, and Kessa couldn't wait. As soon as Toria picked up, the words tumbled out of Kessa's mouth like marbles pouring out of a pouch.

"He kissed me! I had my first kiss! And my second too. It just happened and I don't even know if I was doing it right, but it felt right—you know what I mean? Well, I definitely didn't do it right the first time, but none of that matters," she squealed. "I kissed a boy!"

There was silence on the other end of the line. A silence in which there should have been shrieking and laughter and urgent pleas of "Details, please!" and "Tell me everything."

"I'm really proud of you, Kestha. You're finally growing up." Oddly, Toria's voice sounded younger than it should, and there was a hint of a lisp in her pronunciation.

"What's that supposed to mean?" Kessa shot back as she bolted upright. Her chest felt tight. This wasn't how this conversation was supposed to go. And what gave Toria the right to be "proud" of her anyway? As if she was just some lost little girl, finally finding her way out of the woods.

"Well, you haven't thstarted your monthly cycles yet, so kisthing a boy isth progressth for you."

"It's not a race, and having a period doesn't make you any more grown up than me—we're the same age. Besides, who crowned you Miss Puberty anyway?" More silence, and Kessa could hear Audrina fussing and shrieking in the background on the other end. "You were the one who pressured me into finding a crush in the first place, so why are you acting like this?"

"Listhen, Kestha, I have to go. I need to help Audrina. I'll talk to you later."

The initial anger and confusion subsided as Kessa put down the phone, and a completely new emotion, a soothing one, blew in to ease her heated feelings.

Her eyes drifted down to where her legs were hanging off the bed. She hadn't shaved since before her hike with Arthur, and she never even noticed until now that the hair had grown back. It wasn't any darker or thicker. It was no different than it had been before.

Toria may have had her period first, but Kessa had the first kiss, no matter how unfair it might seem to Toria. She had something that Toria didn't, and somehow that made it all the more special, like a rare gem, something secret and sparkling for only her to treasure.

Chapter 29: Millie

Four days had gone by and Kessa had not heard from Toria. She had sent messages to their shared text thread with Maddy, but only Maddy had replied. It wasn't her fault if Toria was mad at her. She didn't even know why things had gone wrong. Toria had been constantly annoyed with her during the school year for not being boy crazy enough, and now that Kessa had finally developed a crush on someone—and even had that all-important, notable first kiss—Toria refused to talk to her.

Kessa studied her reflection in the mirror and gathered her hair into a ponytail. The elastic popped off her hand and landed in the corner of the room next to a medium-sized Tupperware container. She reached out and grabbed the container, clutching it to her chest as she braced against the swelling tidal wave of grief that washed over her.

The last time Kessa had been to the sanctuary, Ruth had sent her home with homemade dog biscuits for Bucky. Kessa had never given him the biscuits, not one—she had forgotten about them. That she hadn't remembered the treats, treats he would have enjoyed, absolutely crushed her.

The pain she had been feeling for the last few days started up again. Not just the grief she felt for Bucky, but the cramping sensation below her stomach—it was becoming more and more uncomfortable, and now her lower back felt sore as well. She thought about staying home in bed, but for today, she resolved that she would just have to suck it up, because she was going to the sanctuary for the last time this summer, and she wanted to say goodbye to Ruth.

She had also told Millie that she would take her along so they could have some special time together, just the two of them, without Arthur. It was a plan that had come together on the way home from the dance, when Kessa had taken ahold of Millie's hand in the back seat of the Range Rover and made the promise. Millie's tears had evaporated quickly in the hot, rushing wind that roared through the rolled-down windows.

That night had been charged with more than swing music and heated twilight. Something about it stuck in her mind. Maybe it was Needra's intoxicating perfume or the way it felt to glide across the floor in that pine-scented community hall. Or maybe it was Millie's eyes, the way they had burned through her before she ran out, or the way Arthur's words had left her throat clogged in the thick night air, there on the curb beneath the streetlight. All of it still rolled around in her mind like something boiling on a forgotten burner.

As her dad waited with Millie in the car, Kessa ran to take one last trip to the bathroom, and that was when it happened. It was just a red spot on the toilet paper, but the sight of it filled her with a mixture of shock and relief. She had known this was coming, and she had expected it to happen at the lake, but suddenly she didn't feel at all prepared.

She tore through her dresser drawers until she found the plastic zip case that her mom had packed for her, then raced back into the bathroom. The case held a bunch of plastic-wrapped pads, an array of tampons, and a small baggie with a little plastic cup in it.

Way too many options.

She unwrapped one of the pads and tried to stick it in her underwear correctly, but when she pulled everything up, it felt like the pad was resting more on her behind than anywhere else. She readjusted the pad, unsticking it and sticking it again until it felt like it was in the right position, and then stuffed some extra ones into her backpack before running out the door.

"What took you so long?" Millie whined as Kessa climbed into the back seat next to her.

"Nothing, Millipede, nothing. I just forgot something."

Millie smiled and grabbed Kessa's hand as "Hey Jude" came one. "I know all the lyrics to this one—all of them!"

Kessa laughed. "Me too."

Millie sang at the top of her lungs, and as the chorus swelled, Kessa felt a pulling in her heart like the moon wrestling with the tide. With each refrain, the song released her a little bit more, sending her mind up, up, and away into the clouds.

She was lighter than air.

• • •

As always, toward the end of August, the cicadas buzzed louder than ever, and though the nights were starting to become a little bit cooler, the heat of the day continued to soar into the high eighties with the noon sun.

Kessa and Millie stopped to say hi to Lola first after arriving at the sanctuary. Ruth had set up a huge enclosure for her and had also taken on two other alpacas that needed care so that Lola wouldn't have to be alone. It had a nice shady spot too, and Kessa was so relieved Lola wouldn't have to suffer anymore. She thought about going into the enclosure to give Lola a big hug, but she didn't want to spook the newcomers. After giving the alpacas the carrot and apple pieces they'd brought, Kessa and Millie trudged up to the barn and walked through it, out the back opening, and right into a massive gathering of chickens.

"Wow! I've never seen this many chickens here before!" Millie said.

Ruth was sitting on an old stump and scattering feed for them. She looked more tired than usual probably because she didn't have enough volunteers coming during the week to help out. It was common for volunteers to not show up when the temperature rose too high. A part of Kessa wished she could stay longer and help Ruth around the sanctuary into the fall.

"These chickens were part of a school hatching program," Ruth said. "At the end of the year, if none of the kids or parents take the chicks home, they get sent back to the farm where they came from. The kids never want to do that, of course, because they've had time to bond with them." Ruth sighed and shook her head. "And, well, the farm handles them the way a farm always will, but once one school heard that I would take their chicks, others got the word and came to drop theirs off before summer vacation started. Now I've got all of these lovelies to keep me company." She chuckled. "What I'll do if they bring me more next year, I don't know!"

Millie helped Ruth and Kessa scatter the feed and then asked if she could go see the horses. When they got to the fence at the edge of the pasture, Millie hoisted herself up to get a better look and pointed at Jersey, who was lying peacefully under the shade of the cottonwood tree. "Hey, look! A new cow!"

"Actually, it's a bull." Kessa smiled and sent a kind thought over to Jersey as he gave his tail a lazy flick. *You look relaxed.*

"Ruth, can I ride one of those horses over there?" Millie pointed at Rig and Willa, who were standing side by side out in the field, swishing their tails.

"Rig and Willa had a hard life before they came to the sanctuary. They're here to rest and relax, not give rides," Kessa said.

• • •

After bringing a few loads of vegetables to the farm stand and tending to the animals in the barn, Millie began to whine that she was hungry, to which Ruth replied, with a glint in her eye, "Oh, do I have a treat for you!" She sent them off to wait at the picnic table while she went inside to get the food.

Millie jiggled her legs beneath the weather-worn wooden table as they waited for the food, and Kessa made sure to look out for splinters as she sat down. Millie had her Cat's Cradle string, and the two of them played for a bit until they spotted Ruth heading toward them. She was holding a silver pot and had an old-fashioned picnic basket hanging from the crook of her arm.

Ruth set the pot down and withdrew the cover with a flourish.

"These are bean-hole beans!"

"What's a bean hole?" Millie asked, leaning over the table to peer into the pot.

"Bean-hole beans are a tradition of my people. The early settlers learned how to make this dish from us. Some of my friends came to stay here a few nights ago, and they helped dig out the hole to cook them in."

"These beans were baked in the ground?"

Ruth smiled. "Yes, in a big pit. Cooking them this way gives them a taste like no other. You'll see," she said as she scooped out a bowl of cold beans for each of them. "I'm going to leave you girls to eat. I have some things I need to do in the greenhouse. Help yourself to the lemonade." She withdrew a large, clear thermos from the picnic basket and set it out on the table. Kessa could see that it was filled with Ruth's own homemade lemonade and was filled to the brim with ice cubes.

Millie inhaled her beans and reached into the pot to dish out some more. "Who ever thought that cold beans cooked in a hole in the ground would be so délicieux?"

"Okay, Fancy Nancy," Kessa said with a smirk. "Ruth always makes good stuff." She laid her spoon down as Millie gobbled up her second helping. "Hey, I just wanted to say, I'm sorry about how things have gone this summer. I never meant to exclude you. Really. Arthur told me about your dad leaving too. That's a lot to deal with."

Millie looked up and pushed her bowl away into the center of the table, her mouth set into a thin, hard line. "It's fine."

"No, it's not. I know what it's like to feel left out, especially when there's a group of three friends. It can be really easy for someone to get sidelined."

Kessa remembered when she and Toria had first started including Maddy when they did things, like going to the mall or meeting after school to do homework. One day, after they had all regularly been hanging out as a trio, Toria had invited just Maddy over to her house for dinner. Toria had posted pictures of the two of them goofing around upstairs in her bedroom, having fun, just being together—without Kessa.

Even though she eventually realized they were not intentionally trying to exclude her, it never got any easier to see the two of them together without her, and she wondered if it ever would. She had been careful to not be on social media too much during her time at the lake because she knew that if she saw pictures of Toria and Maddy hanging out, she would feel a fire inside like a belly full of glowing hot ash.

"I wish Daisy was old enough to play with me. All I have is Arthur and my books, and now you're leaving." Millie tugged at the elastics on her wrist, pulling and snapping them until she flinched.

"She will be, someday," Kessa said. "She's already talking a lot, even more now than when I first got here."

"She wrecks my blanket forts."

"Why don't we build a new one together, an even bigger and better one?"

Millie's eyebrows popped up. "Really? Okay! We have to do it today or tomorrow, though, because you're leaving soon."

"It's a plan! I promise we'll do it before I go." Kessa stood up and began tidying the table so they could carry the things to Ruth's back porch.

Millie held up a spoon and examined her reflection. She turned the spoon by the handle and tilted her head. "It's weird to have someone just go away, especially when you're so used to them being around."

"Oh, you don't have to worry about that, Mill. You know I'd never miss a summer at the lake. I'll be back next year for sure."

Millie lowered the spoon and placed it on the table with care.

"I didn't mean you."

Chapter 30: A Parallel Universe

"Toria!"

Kessa ran down the porch steps, surprised to see her best friend standing beside the hammock in the front yard.

"Hi, Graham." Kessa's mom greeted her dad with a hug at the door and gave him a peck on the cheek.

"C'mon in, Marg. Are you hungry? We made vegan enchiladas." Her parents' voices disappeared behind the screen door as it banged shut, and Kessa watched Toria's eyes dart around the yard. Over the lake, the sun made a twilight glow as it began to dip below the horizon.

"This place is awesome." Toria climbed into the hammock and lay back so that she was looking up into the lush canopy of the trees. A warm breeze rushed through the leaves, and Kessa breathed it in, inhaling the heady smell of the late August night.

"How many people do you think can fit on this thing?"

Kessa stepped out of her flip-flops and got in next to her. "At least two. I can't believe you came!"

"I thought it would be cool to surprise you. Besides, I've been dying to see this place since forever. Like, you have a lake house and I've never been. It's practically a crime."

"It's such a long drive, though. I'm surprised your mom let you go."

"It was your mom's idea. She called my mom and they set it all up." Toria wiggled her toes in her sandals and put her hands behind her head. "This is a great make-out spot. Is this where you kissed that boy?"

"We didn't make out," Kessa said with a laugh. "It happened over there." She threw her arm out over the mesh edge of the hammock and pointed to the swing on the front porch. For a moment, her favorite scene of the summer rushed in, zinging between her ears. It was like they were still over there, she and Arthur, the energy of that moment hanging in the air and buzzing like the crickets. And maybe it was, still burning away in some parallel universe, too flowery to describe. Toria liked things swift and to the point anyway. Most people did. "It was just two quick kisses."

Toria turned onto her side, pressing her hands together and sliding them beneath her cheek. Kessa could smell her hair when she shifted to face her. It was a fresh, juicy smell. Toria wasn't wearing any mascara or eye makeup; she looked just like the Toria of the Special Six Club, the Toria who had fit right beside her in the beanbag chair in kindergarten, the Toria who had asked Kessa to comb her hair with her fingers when they were in first grade just because she liked how it felt.

"Can I meet him?" Toria raised her brows imploringly, like a little kid asking for candy.

"Yeah, he'll be around tomorrow." Kessa held her breath for a moment, not sure what to say. It felt weird to have Toria right in front of her after a whole summer of not seeing her. "Did you bring nail polish?" She held out her hand and waved her fingers so Toria could see the ragged edges of her nails, which were dotted with tiny spots of chipped purple polish.

"Of course." Toria's grin gleamed with silver wire.

"You got braces!"

Toria brought her hand to her mouth in a flash and squeezed her eyes shut.

"Why didn't you tell me? Does it hurt? Let me see!" Kessa reached over and pried her hand away from her mouth.

"It was hard to talk with them at first. I sounded so stupid." Toria scrunched her eyes closed, knitting her brows together. "It looks awful. I can't even chew gum. Kessa, no boy is ever going to kiss me looking like this!"

"Lots of people have braces. Remember when we were little and we would play that game where we were both teenagers in high school? And we would always pretend those two skinny closets in your hallway were our lockers?"

"Yeah, of course."

"And remember how we tried to tape pieces of floss across our teeth so it would look like we had braces because we thought it would make us look like real teenagers? Well, now you are a teenager, and you don't want the one thing that makes you look legit!" Kessa sucked in her giggles like a hyena.

Toria let out a completely natural laugh. It was a brilliant chime of bells in the growing twilight, but it was immediately smothered because she closed her mouth again, pressing her lips tight together. She inhaled a deep breath through her nose and fixed her eyes somewhere beyond the house where the lake lay dark and cool beneath the stars.

"I have to have my first kiss before I turn sixteen. Otherwise, it will be too late, and I have to have these braces on for at least three years."

"Too late? Too late for what?"

"Kessa, everyone should have their first kiss by sixteen. It would be pathetic not to. It's practically a rule."

"Who says?"

"It's just a rule!" Toria shot back.

Sippy's view of the lake filtered through Kessa's mind. Like a movie camera sailing through the sky, she could see herself down below, leaning on her right arm into the netting of the hammock, her light blue flip-flops on the ground like two pale smudges in the dirt. It felt like a scene she might read in a book. No, this was something she could write. Maybe she could even win that contest after all. But she would never have a chance if she didn't send it in.

Kessa leaned in and gave Toria a peck on the cheek, then dropped her head back with a giggle.

"There ya go!" Kessa exclaimed. "Now you don't have to worry about anything." She continued in a Shakespearian tone, "Thou hath been kissethed before thee age of sixteen." Kessa had been feeling like a new person lately, like extra electricity was buzzing somewhere between her throat and her chest, and it felt silly and impulsive and daring to help out Toria with this "problem" of hers.

"You're nuts! It doesn't count if it's on the cheek. Or from another girl." Toria stuck her tongue out between her decorated teeth and then grinned.

"Well, it should," Kessa said, tilting her face up to the dark mass of leaves above. For some reason, she thought about the surprise dolls all closed up in a box in Toria's basement. She felt bad for them. Maybe they could play with them again when they brought them back upstairs for Audrina to use. Maybe Toria would set out all their tiny outfits, all the best little shoes and bags and skirts, and tell Kessa to go shopping at her store, one last time, with the plasticky smell lingering on their fingers. Maybe she would still say "excellent choice" at every outfit Kessa chose and smile that same encouraging gap-toothed smile. Or maybe, probably, none of that would ever happen again.

"That small gap between your two front teeth—is that going to go away now because of the braces?"

"I don't know. I think so. Why?"

"Because I like it. I'll miss it."

Toria grabbed Kessa's arm and wrapped hers around it.

"Promise we'll always be best friends?"

"Yes," Kessa whispered as she curled her pinkie finger around Toria's. "Promise."

Chapter 31: Ashes

"Wow, you look so pretty. Are you a model or something?"

Toria sent a bubble of laughter into her hand, which she cupped over her glossy lips. "Can you believe this little chick? How cute is she!"

"I don't want to be cute," Millie said, taking a seat on the lowest front step of the porch. "I want to be pretty. Can you teach me how to be pretty like you?"

"I can paint your nails!"

"Really?" Millie's back straightened as she looked up at Toria hopefully. "What colors do you have?"

"All of them," Kessa said with a laugh. "Let's do it tonight after dinner. We're not leaving until tomorrow."

Kessa and Toria sat shoulder to shoulder on the top step, enjoying the early morning sun and passing infectious yawns back and forth. Toria had wanted to do a séance out on the back porch to try to contact the spirits of the lake and had insisted they do it at midnight or later,

but the last thing Kessa remembered was staring at the clock right before it was about to tick past eleven.

"Hey," Millie said, "do you want to see the garden?"

"Yeah. Let's show her the garden." Kessa stood up and grabbed the watering can at the base of the stairs. "We should pick some tomatoes and take them with us for the drive."

Millie ran ahead while Kessa and Toria stopped by the side of the house to fill up the watering can.

"Is that him?" Toria said in a low whisper, her eyes like laser beams as she looked out across the lawn.

Kessa could see Arthur tromping briskly toward them through the tall grass near the edge of the yard. A slight flutter in her chest sent warmth to her face, and she bent down to turn off the tap. There was a wonderful soreness in her cheeks from trying to keep the corners of her mouth from reaching her ears.

"He's cute!" Toria hissed, slapping Kessa lightly on the shoulder.

"Hi! You must be Toria." Arthur was still catching his breath as he held out his hand to offer Toria a shake. Kessa's heart reeled from the gesture. It was so formal and polite. Her boyfriend, the perfect gentleman. Could she even call him that? Was he her boyfriend?

"Kessa." Arthur gave her a small nod and smiled softly, but his eyes held hers for an extra moment before looking over at the garden. "The tomato plants are looking really great!"

"Yeah, it was being destroyed by a raccoon for a while, I think, but nothing has been eaten lately. Everything has been growing really well."

"Shhhhh!" Millie said as they approached. "There's a squirrel in here, and it's looking right at me!"

Kessa sat down next to Millie, and Mihku winked.

"Did he just wink?" Millie said with an excited whisper. "I think he winked at us!"

"Look!" Toria said. She pointed to something small hopping around the marigolds. "Look at the cute bird."

"It's a little sips," Arthur said, tilting his head to the side and taking a seat next to Kessa on the ground. "She doesn't seem afraid of us at all."

Kessa jerked her head up and looked at Arthur with narrowed eyes. "What did you just say?"

"Sips? It's an Algonquian word for little birds like that. I'm sure you've heard me say it before. Sometimes I call them Sippies."

"Hold up, you speak a Native American language?" Toria flipped her hair back as Mihku scurried over to Arthur's shoes and sniffed at them.

"Not bad, not bad at all. Hardly any smell," Mihku said. Only Kessa heard it, of course. She clapped her hand over her mouth to stifle her laughter.

Arthur held still while Mihku explored his boots with quivering whiskers. "I am by no means fluent, but I'm familiar with a handful of the Penobscot and Passamaquoddy words for some common plants and animals that are native to here. The Algonquian language is really fascinating."

"Passamawhat?" Toria leaned over, plucked a small red cherry tomato off the vine, and popped it into her mouth.

"It's all part of the history of this area. Maine is made up of five major tribes: Mi'kmaq, Maliseet, Penobscot, Passamaquoddy, and Abenaki. All of them, here in Maine and up into Nova Scotia, make up the Wabanaki Confederacy."

"Yeah, that's why this place is called Lake Wabanaki," Millie said quietly as she held out her hands for Sippy, who was hopping closer to investigate the colorful elastic bands around her wrists. "It means 'People of the Dawnland.'"

Toria sat on her knees and looked from Arthur to Millie without batting her lashes once. "Kess, didn't you say these two have never been to school?"

Kessa giggled and nudged Arthur with her elbow. "Yeah, I told you they were smart."

All of the sudden there was a ruffle of feathers, and Sippy shot up into the sky. Almost simultaneously, Mihku dashed across the garden bed and headed down the hill where he disappeared beneath the back porch as Candice's tall, slender frame in a long flowing sundress cut across the lawn, with Daisy on her hip.

"Awww!" Millie cried. "That little bird was just about to step right into my hands! Did you see that, guys? Did you see?"

Candice put Daisy down and let her toddle through the grass. "Kessa, who is your lovely friend?"

"This is Toria," Kessa said, then added, "We've been best friends since kindergarten. Toria's also an artist."

"Ah!" Candice tucked her chin in as if peering over invisible spectacles. "I should show you my studio. I'd absolutely love to have you over for a critique."

Daisy clambered into the garden bed and began pulling at leaves. "Dizzy has Kissy's fowers?"

"No, no, Daisy, you can't do that." Arthur stood up and gently pried a marigold out of her fist before she could snap it off.

"I have fowers now?" Daisy looked up at Kessa, her big gray eyes pleading. Kessa guided her little hands to the handle of the watering can so she could "help" water the plants.

"Look at you, Daisy, watering the garden like a big girl," Candice said in a crooning voice. "You're so good with her, Kessa. Would you like to babysit next summer? I'll pay you, of course."

"Sure!" Kessa's eyes darted over to Toria, who smiled and held a thumbs-up close to her chest.

"Anyway," Candice said, "your parents called and said I should come over now because you're going to be spreading Bucky's ashes soon." Her hair cascaded freely down her back as she closed her eyes and pointed her freckled face up into the sun. She drew in a long, deep, exaggerated breath and reached up to the sky. "Couldn't ask for a more perfect day either."

"Mom, it's a memorial for Bucky, not a yoga retreat." Arthur looked at the ground, bugging out his eyes and shaking his head, but Kessa had already thought about the weather. It was too sunny a backdrop for the sadness she was going to have to confront. It still didn't feel right to be happy, to feel okay, to go on with the day like she always had before. She wondered if it ever would.

. . .

After they had received Bucky's ashes, it had been her dad's idea to wait for her mom to come up so she could be there when they sprinkled the remains into the lake before going back home. Kessa stared out over the lake, waiting for her next breath to save her. When she glanced to her side, she saw that Toria was looking at her, and even with the sharp black liner, her brown eyes looked about as kind and soft as Bucky's had been as a young puppy.

As they gathered around the dock, Kessa's dad pulled the plastic bag of ashes out of the urn and urged Kessa to make the first statement. She hadn't prepared anything in writing like he had suggested, so the words just sort of fell from her mouth as her brain struggled to catch up with all the things her heart had been longing to say.

"Bucky, my summers here would have never been the same without you. You've been with me for as long as I can remember. You were my first true friend." She paused briefly and swallowed the lump in her throat. "If I had thought you weren't going to survive the surgery, I never would have encouraged Dad to bring you to the vet to have it done. If I had known it was so dangerous, I would have gone so I could be with you." Her eyes welled up and her heart beat raggedly as if threatening to burst through her ribs. "I . . . I should have been there." She began choking on each word as they rolled up her throat, but she pressed on. "I would give anything to kiss your head again and to feel your soft ears. Bucky, I hope you are at peace now. I'll never forget you. Never."

Her dad had told her this wasn't her fault, that the vet had explained how bad Bucky's eyes had been, that the risk of the surgery had been necessary to try to alleviate his pain, and that, ultimately, it had been Bucky's time to go, but none of that had made the grief any easier to bear.

"Bucky? If you can hear me, I didn't know that the last time I saw you was going to be the last time." She didn't want Bucky to think she didn't care. The thought of it shredded her up inside, and she'd been twisting her sheets in agony every night since he had been gone.

"I'm sorry. I'm so sorry I never got a chance to say goodbye to you." She drew a fistful of ashes from the bag and cast them out over the lake. The bright morning light bouncing off the surface caused her watery eyes to squint and leak even more, but she could still see that the spot where the ashes fell to the water held a soft rainbow glow. Moxie was there and gave her the courage she needed to finish her eulogy. "I loved you more than any girl could ever love a dog. I still love you and I always will."

Her mom moved forward on the dock and hugged Kessa from behind, wrapping her arms around her waist.

"Can I do some?" Millie stood up and dipped her hand into the bag. "Ashes to ashes and dust to dust, and now, ashes to lake. Bucky, you will be a part of this lake forever. Goodbye. We love you." She threw out a fistful of ashes, and the small gray cloud dissipated over the lake's shimmering surface. Millie then passed the bag to Arthur.

"Bucky, I hope you are reincarnated into a new animal so that you can stay living near the lake, but we have made so many good memories with you over the years that you will live on in our hearts no matter what. May you find peace, wherever you are." Arthur knelt down on one knee before the edge of the dock and carefully sprinkled some ashes over the rippling water.

"Graham? Are you going to say something?" Kessa's mom pulled her dad toward them by the back of his arm. With a fumbling hand, he reached into his back pocket and withdrew a neatly folded-up piece of paper.

"I named him Lucky because I thought he was a lucky little dog when I rescued him from the adoption center, but I soon learned that I was the one who was lucky to have him. Like my daughter, who gave him the name that stuck, Bucky's presence changed my life for the better.

"Bucky was a living example to me that nonhuman animals deserve as much love and compassion as any human being. Not just the animals we choose as pets and invite into our families, but all animals, and I . . ." He dropped his arm, paper in hand, and looked out over the lake. "I turned a blind eye to that for far too long, but Kessa never gave up on me. She constantly urged me to see in a new light. I just wish I had made the connection sooner. In the name of Bucky and all living creatures, I choose to continue my life in as peaceful a way as possible by doing the least amount of harm possible. From this day forward, I choose to live the vegan way."

A vision of her own heart rippled through Kessa as she reached out and hugged her dad. There were so many ways to describe it, but the colors came first. It was purple and wet and wrung out, but also, it was strong and red and rushing, like one long, continuous, and beautiful alliteration. It was just life, and she could feel it as fully as the tears on her face, the tears she didn't bother to hide, because it was okay to cry now, even on dry land.

Arthur held out the bag, and with a trembling smile, her dad scooped out a small handful of ashes. He sent the gray dust raining over the lake with one powerful thrust from his shoulder. "I'm so grateful to have had you in my life." The way that his voice dwindled to a strangled whisper at the end caused a crack in Kessa's tender heart. It was as if it was physically breaking, but somehow she knew that, while it was breaking, it was opening up too, in a bloody and flowery sort of way.

Standing there between her mother and father, she thought about how different her life would have been if they had never divorced, if her dad had never bought the old crooked lake house that stood behind her. Everything, absolutely everything, would be different. There would have been no dock, no Bucky, no first kiss on the porch swing, and no summer when her dad decided to stop eating animals for good.

Suddenly Daisy looked up from where she had been quietly sitting on Candice's lap and clapped her hands. "I do asses too?"

Millie erupted in a high-pitched squeal and then quickly clapped her hands over her mouth.

"Asses, asses! Asses to Dizzy now? I do it! I do it!"

Toria, who had stood with her head bowed solemnly throughout the whole ceremony, looked over at Kessa with her mouth hanging open. They went into complete convulsions, and Kessa's mom couldn't help but chuckle with them. The laughter spread around the dock as her dad leaned over and opened the bag for Daisy to stick her fist in. The ashes mostly sifted through her clenched hand before she threw them, her arm stretched out as she opened her fingers like a tiny firework. "Bucky, wuv you!"

As they turned to leave the dock, Kessa looked up at the back porch, and there, high up on the railing, looking out at the lake, a small bird was perched near a fat squirrel. They just looked like your average brown sparrow and ordinary wild squirrel, and she had to smile to herself because she knew that they were anything but.

Chapter 32: Maybe

Millie had decided that she wanted each of her nails painted a different color, like a rainbow. Toria did the whole spa routine, which included soaking their hands in warm water, pushing down the cuticles, filing, buffing, and mini hand massages. She also gave both Millie and Kessa facials with cucumber slices over their eyes. The whole nine, as Toria liked to say. The cucumbers kept slipping off, which sent Millie into repeated giggling fits. Before it was time for her to leave, they ate the rest of the cucumber slices while staring at their flushed and dewy faces in the mirror.

"Can't I sleep here tonight with you guys?" Millie asked, running her hand over her smooth, freshly pampered cheek.

"Sorry, li'l chica, we'll be up way past your bedtime," Toria said matter-of-factly.

Millie puffed out her lower lip and her eyes took on a glossy shine. Kessa reached out and hugged her, folding her in like a mother hen. Millie's shoulders jumped inside the embrace, and Kessa held her tighter as Millie began gasping with feeble, wounded cries.

"Please, please don't leave, Kessa. Please." She buried her face into Kessa's shirt, which hardly muffled the sobs.

Kessa caught the alarmed look that flickered across Toria's face and then watched as she ran to the dresser and began gathering up a variety of colored polishes. "Here, you can keep these—just take them. Now you can do your nails anytime."

"We'll make sure to say goodbye before we leave tomorrow morning, okay?" Kessa said, taking Millie's face in her hands. She almost felt like crying herself.

Millie hiccupped and held out the bottom of her T-shirt for Toria to drop the colors into as Kessa stepped back. Kessa accidently bit down on her freshy painted thumbnail, but Toria swatted her hand away before she was able to do too much damage.

"Thanks for the colors," Millie said, casting an empty gaze at the bottles in her shirt pouch. She drew in a long, shivering breath and looked up at Kessa, a startling amount of pain crinkling up the corners of her eyes. "What if my dad never comes back?"

Kessa and Toria exchanged glances, each of their faces searching the other's for answers. They waited for some kind of wisdom to offer, some words of support or even a worn-out platitude, but nothing came. A heart-aching silence clung to the air, and their gazes drifted downward, as if they could see Millie's hope falling like a feather.

"Maybe they just need some time to work things out," Kessa offered, her words a desperate current of air rushing out to keep the feather afloat.

"Maybe," Millie whispered, her tears falling onto the shiny bottles. She sniffled as she turned to the door.

"Hey, wait," Toria said, rummaging in her bag at the foot of the bed. "It's dark out now. You should take this."

Toria switched on a small plastic votive candle and placed it into Millie's shirt on top of the polishes. "You can keep it. I have, like, twenty of these."

Millie gave Toria a quizzical look and Kessa laughed. "We were going to do a séance last night, but we fell asleep too soon.

We're going to try again tonight."

"Like contacting ghosts?" Millie asked, her eyes growing wide. "I've always wanted to try that."

"Spirits, yes. My aunt is a professional medium." Toria turned to Kessa. "I bet she would like Paranormal Perpetrators, but she's probably too little."

"Yeah. It might be scary for her, and it is getting late."

"No! I don't get scared that easy," Millie protested.

"Well, you better hurry home, then," Toria said, glancing over to where the digital clock sat on the dresser, obscured by a small heap of damp face cloths from the spa treatments. "It starts soon, I think."

"Okay," Millie said. "And I can stay up as late as I want. Just so you know." She sniffed and licked a drip of wetness off her upper lip. "I'm not a baby—I'm almost ten. And you guys should really come over tomorrow. Candice cleaned the whole house It's really nice. She even made dinner for us every night this past week!"

"We'll try to, okay?" Kessa said, relived to hear that Candice had been keeping up the house. Ever since the incident with Daisy, Candice had been acting like a super mom. She had always been a little flighty, but now she seemed to be taking action and making a real effort. Kessa just hoped, for Arthur, Millie, and Daisy's sake, it would last.

Toria closed the door behind Millie and leaned her back against it. "That was intense."

"Yeah. But you were really sweet with her. I think you have a way with kids. You should come back next year and help me babysit Daisy. You heard Candice—she's going to pay me. We could split it. You'll obviously be more experienced because you have Audrina at home."

"Yeah, maybe." Toria took a seat on the edge of the bed and looked up at the seashell clock on the wall. "Can you keep a secret?"

"Of course. You can tell me anything."

"I can't tell time on round clocks. Like, I have no idea unless it's digital."

"Are you serious?"

"Yeah, I'm not joking."

Kessa looked at the cloths covering the digital clock and felt a wild, playful tingle zap through her. She didn't want to be mean, but it was a little bit fun to tease, and she just couldn't resist. "What time is it now?" She bit her lower lip as it curved into a smile and raised her eyebrows up and down like a cartoon villain with a plan.

"Stop it!"

"Look at the seashell clock on the wall." She pointed at it. "Just try."

"Kess, I told you, I can't. I could stare at it for ten minutes and still not figure it out." She snorted out a laugh and leaned back into the bed.

"I guess I can let you off this time," Kessa said before taking a running jump and landing on her knees atop the bed, "but I'm going to help you. It's easier than you think." The bed made a sagging dent in the middle of the mattress, which Toria rolled into, laughing and peeking through her fingers like a little kid counting for hide-and-seek. "So, are you going to tell Maddy this deep, dark secret of your soul?"

Toria moved her hands away from her face and looked up at the ceiling as if she could see all the stars of the night right through it. Her mouth split into a sharky grin. "Maybe."

"Maybe, maybe, maybe. May. Be." Kessa stuck her tongue out between her teeth. "It sounds so weird if you say it too much. Try it!"

"Maybe, maybe, maybe, baby, baby, maybe!"

They burst into fits of giggles, and Kessa turned onto her side, holding her ribs. The window was wide open, and the curtains stretched out on the breeze. She wondered if the spirits of the lake could hear their laughter and their secrets. She could almost make out their forms rising from the water like steam curling up toward the moon. Fragile, silver wisps of smoke in the night. Maybe they were watching. Maybe, maybe.

Chapter 33: Dark Sunshine

The digital clock, now cleared of messy obstructions, displayed the time brightly, the numbers emanating a green shine that reflected against the smooth top of the dresser. It was eleven forty-five, and midnight was closing in rapidly. The spirits of the lake were probably drifting in and out of the mist, aimless souls just waiting for a couple of teenagers to come along and ask them questions. What else did they have to do anyway?

"Do you think the spirits will want to talk about how they died?" Kessa whispered. The sound of Toria's measured breaths made Kessa sleepy, but she fought it, squinting her eyes until the glowing numbers blurred together.

"Probably," Toria said. She rolled onto her stomach and let out a sigh. "I like the wallpaper in here. It reminds me of the wallpaper in my old dollhouse."

"Oh, yeah. It really does," Kessa said, her voice cracking through a whisper. "I knew there was a reason I loved that dollhouse so much."

They were quiet for a few minutes, and Kessa pulled the covers up to her chin. She liked having Toria in the room with her. There was a certain wordless comfort in hearing someone else's familiar breathing in the dark. It was a silent togetherness that she could wrap around her like a blanket, something worn in and quilted and safe. She could feel the weight of it and wondered if this was what it was like to have a sister. A sister to hush the words when it got too late and then soak up all the secrets that didn't need to be said because everything had already been shared.

"Toria," she began, testing her wakefulness with a soft tone, "do you ever feel like a bad person or wonder if something . . ." She paused as Toria turned over in the bed. "If something is kind of wrong with you because maybe you don't always have the nicest thoughts?"

Toria rustled against the pillow, folding her arms behind her head. "Actually, since you asked, I think my heart is a bit wicked, honestly."

"Wicked heart? Really?" Kessa propped herself up on her elbow so that she was facing Toria, an impish smile on her lips. "Would you say your heart is like . . . the dark sunshine of a total solar eclipse?"

"What?"

Kessa let her head fall back onto the pillow and let out a one-breath laugh. "I just like to think of ways to describe things. It's a thing I do in my head. I probably shouldn't say that stuff out loud. I sound nutty."

"No, you sound like a poet without enough paper, and I love it."

"Poet without enough paper." She nodded, eyes flicking up to the darkened face of the seashell clock. "That's a good one. So, why do you have a wicked heart? Why do you think you're a bad person?"

"Well, lots of times I get this feeling, but it's totally wrong and bad. It's called schadenfreude. I think it's German."

"Describe it," Kessa said, studying the fine, crooked cracks that spread like a road map across the ceiling.

"Okay." Toria looked up and ran her tongue across the braces on her front teeth. "I'll give you an example. Lilyette Lane."

"Oh. I hate her."

"I know, right? So, you know how she's always been pretty? Like, almost too pretty?"

"Way too pretty."

"And you know how mean she was to me when we were in third and fourth grade."

Kessa recalled the many times Lilyette had bullied Toria. Not that Toria was always sweet and innocent, but she certainly didn't deserve what Lilyette had done. One time, Lilyette had spread a rumor that Toria was a witch, which Toria actually liked at first, until all the kids at recess one day decided that because she was a witch, she could give you a toad disease if you went near her. For weeks, all the kids would run away screaming if she so much as blinked in their direction.

"Anyway, a few weeks ago, I ran into her at the grocery store with my mom, and she had terrible acne all over her face. Not just regular pimples either—the bumpy kind that make big red welts and leave scars. I was shook."

"Wow, that's awful."

"I know. But that's the thing. I didn't feel bad for her. I mean, I did in one way, but in another way, I actually felt kind of cheered up. It's not supposed to feel good when something bad happens to someone. It's—"

"Dark sunshine," Kessa said.

"Yes. But it does make me feel better that there's a word for it, even if it is German, so that means I'm not the only one to feel this. Maybe people just don't talk about it. Because who would, right? It's horrible."

"It's not so bad," Kessa said, leaning onto her elbow again. "I get what you're saying."

"And since we're on the topic of my wicked heart, I'm sorry how I acted before on the phone. You were excited about your kiss with Arthur and I should have been more supportive."

"I was a little confused," Kessa admitted. "At least, it wasn't the reaction I expected." She studied Toria's profile in the dark for moment, hoping to see how remorse would look on her face.

"I know. I just had the braces put on. It was hard to talk and I sounded ridiculous, and they hurt too, and every time I looked in the mirror, I felt like they were ruining my face, even with my mouth closed. They're just so ugly."

"So that's why you didn't want to talk? Because of the braces?"

"Well, yes and no. I was upset that you got kissed before me. It didn't feel fair because I've been dealing with this"—Toria pressed her eyes shut and shook her hands in front of her chest—"and everything else for so long. Do you know how hard it was to get my period when I was eleven? I was still playing with the dollhouse then. I didn't want it. I didn't want all this stuff happening to me, but it just did. So, I guess there was this tiny part of me that felt like I deserved to get the first kiss, like I earned it, you know? And you didn't do anything to earn it. I mean, you don't even wear makeup! I'm not making any sense, am I?"

"No, it makes perfect sense."

"It does?" Toria rolled to her side and propped up on her elbow. Kessa could smell the toothpaste on her breath.

"Yes. It's a weird kind of jealousy that I call 'the Burn.' I thought I was the only one who got this feeling. I always have it when people have good things happening to them if I feel they don't deserve it."

"Huh. It's like schadenfreude but different. Maybe there's even a word for it that we don't know about, in a different language. I mean, there really should be, but just because there isn't a word for it doesn't mean it's not a true feeling. It's still totally valid even if it does make you feel a bit mean inside."

"I think everyone must have some parts about themselves that they don't like. Except for Annie. Remember that time when we watched Annie, the movie, in theater club? "

Toria nodded.

"You know that part where she's going to get sent back to her parents and she doesn't want to take all those nice new dresses with her? Instead, she wants to give them away to all her friends back at the orphanage. I would have taken them with me. One hundred percent. Maybe I would give one to my best friend or something—I would save a dress for you—but not the whole dang orphanage. Annie is so selfless. I wish I was more like that."

Toria flashed her braces in a wicked grin. "Nobody is that good and sweet, except for maybe Maddy." She gave a breathy laugh and leaned closer, dropping her voice a bit lower. "I would have taken the dresses with me too."

"So, you don't think I'm a bad person?"

Toria shook her head. "Even if we are a little bit bad, I don't care. It's just spice. My aunt says that all sugar and no spice is boring."

"You think I have spice?"

"Obviously. You know, we're more alike than you think."

"That's kind of funny, because I was afraid you would become better friends with Maddy while I was here this summer and that you wouldn't like me as much anymore."

"That would never happen, Kess. You're too special and you've known me, like, forever. Anyway, Maddy would never hate Lilyette for me. I told her not to invite Lilyette to her birthday party last year, but she did anyway. She also doesn't believe my aunt is a real psychic. She doesn't get me like you do." She paused for a beat. "Nobody does."

Kessa's eyes slid over to the clock. "Eleven fifty-seven." She held on to Toria's arm and gave it a squeeze. "I think we're going to make it."

"Actually, I have to tell you something." Toria fell back onto her pillow and tucked the covers around her waist. She pushed a thin ribbon of air between her lips, the shadows settling into her complexion like a midnight tan. "To be honest, I don't really know how to do a séance. My aunt isn't even going to let me sit in on one until I'm older. It probably wouldn't work anyway."

"Oh. Well, that's okay. I'm kind of exhausted, to tell you the truth." Kessa scooted under the covers and tucked her arms by her sides. It felt awkward and corpse-like. Even after a whole summer, she still wasn't used to sleeping without Chuck Chuck. It was like she didn't know what to do with her arms in bed without the stuffed animal to hug. She curled up on her right side and rubbed at the tops of her knees. "Do you ever get these weird shooting pains in your legs?"

"Yeah," Toria said. The blanket pulled against Kessa's waist as Toria settled into her position on the other side of the bed. "I used to. My mom always said it was just growing pains. And you really need to stop talking now so we can get some rest."

"What about the spirits?" Kessa said, hugging the edge of the bed, the heat of her exhalation warming the sheet beneath her cheek. But Toria didn't reply, and Kessa didn't bother to look at the clock. Somehow she could feel, in the depth of the shadows against the wall and in the rhythm of Toria's breath, that they had made it.

Chapter 34: Wind

The birds outside her window were making such a racket that Kessa rose at dawn and was unable to fall back asleep. Careful not to wake Toria, she rolled out of the bed softly and got dressed in the hallway. After brushing her teeth, she crept downstairs to the writing nook and pulled up the final draft of her story. The contest submissions were due that afternoon at four o'clock, but since she was going to be in the car all day on her way back to Rhode Island, she knew she had to submit it before leaving.

She felt a sense of relief and excitement rush through her fingertips as she hit the submit button and was about to log out of her account when she noticed an unopened email from Toria at the bottom of the screen. It was sent the evening of her birthday, but she hadn't checked her email all summer. She opened it and read through the descriptions of the different planetary placements in her astrological birth chart. Most of the descriptions were fairly similar to each other but the one at the end stood out.

Those with Mars in Aries have an abundance of passion and rarely shy away from a challenge. They can be seen as impulsive, headstrong, and risky but are truthful, confident, courageous, and driven, with a knack for taking matters into their own hands. The energy behind Mars in Aries is assertive rather than passive, and these people are known for their ability to sieze opportunities and not simply lie around waiting for things to happen. They have an adventurous spirit and will never stand idly by when action is required. They can be daring and put their plans into action quickly, often motivated by a competitive spirit or desire for justice.

If she had read that back when Toria had sent it, she would have written off astrology altogether. It would have sounded too inaccurate. Not just inaccurate—impossible. But now it sounded pretty good. Really good.

She had strengths. Thinking of all the adjectives made her smile. Every single one rang true for her now. The spirit of Mars in Aries had been with her when she wanted to help Lola. It had been with her when she jumped the fence to go meet Jersey and when she rescued Daisy. It had been there when she kissed Arthur and even when she allowed herself to cry in front of everyone at Bucky's memorial. Mars in Aries had been in her all along. It was her.

Kessa was still smiling when she wandered into the kitchen, thinking about the strawberries waiting in the fridge—the perfect start to breakfast for her and her friends. As she slipped past the kitchen table, she spied an envelope lying on the countertop with yesterday's mail. It had her name on it and a stamp from the town hall.

The letter was from the mayor's office stating that they appreciated the tips about alternatives to fireworks for the Green Corn Festival and that the town would be looking into celebratory displays that would not be disruptive to the surrounding wildlife. Kessa kissed the letter and did a few quiet twirls in the middle of the kitchen before putting it on the fridge with her favorite picture magnet of Bucky when he was a little pup. She then pulled the bowl of fresh strawberries from the fridge and headed outside, making sure to not let the screen door slam behind her.

"Strawberries! My favorite!" Mihku, as if anticipating her arrival, jumped right into Kessa's lap and rolled a fat strawberry between his paws.

"Where's Sippy?" Kessa tilted her face up into the sky and looked around. The air was cool and damp, and she pulled on the strings at the collar of her hooded sweatshirt.

"She's always gossiping at this time in the morning. You should have heard the racket she was making with her friends!"

"I did," she said with a laugh. "How do you think I was able to meet you out here so early?"

"Listen, Kessa," Mihku said, taking on a serious tone, "as your animal guide, I must warn you that you should handle your gift wisely when you get back home. These powers you have aren't to be used lightly." He bit into his strawberry.

A sudden fluttering of feathers brought Sippy to alight on the edge of the bowl. "Be careful out there, or else you might find you have an awful lot of explaining to do!" she said.

"As long as nothing new comes up, I should be able to manage . . . I think."

"This is only the beginning. You'll learn more things along the way, and we won't always be around to help." Sippy poked her beak into the juicy red flesh of the ripest berry in the bowl.

"More? Like what? I can't get home and have more strange stuff happen to me when I'm least expecting it! You don't understand—I'm starting junior high in a week. I can't hide stuff there easily like I can around the lake."

Sippy paused and looked up. She tilted her head to the side, her dark and beady eye scanning Kessa's worried face. "I'm sorry, Kessa, but there is only so much we can do. Mihku and I are new to being animal guides and we are still learning ourselves."

"But what if something weird happens and I don't know what's going on or how to manage it?"

Mihku shook his head, cheeks packed with strawberries. "You can always call Ruth."

"Ruth?!" Kessa exclaimed.

"Yes. Ruth has the Gift herself, you know. I'm surprised you hadn't figured that out already. I mean, have you seen that greenhouse of hers?"

Kessa dipped her fingers into the bowl and felt somewhat comforted by the fact that Ruth would be able to help guide her, but there was a nagging feeling that told her she was just supposed to handle things on her own. Ruth had probably suspected what was going on after the incidents with the geese and Jersey, but she hadn't said anything. Perhaps she had been waiting for Kessa to say something first. Either way, Ruth had known there was something special about her thirteenth birthday because she had given Kessa that unique stone. It was now packed safely in a pocket on her duffel bag and ready to return home with her. She sampled another strawberry, its sweet flesh bursting on her tongue. She had to savor the company of her friends, as they would not be able to linger for much longer.

Maybe endings were so difficult because, in real life, things didn't really end—they just continued on in one way or another. Maybe last chapters were not so different from new beginnings. She swallowed her bite and asked the question that had been pressing on her mind. "Will you two both be here when I come back next year?"

"Why on earth would you want to come back next year and spend your whole summer stuck out in the middle of nowhere?" Mihku winked at her and then held up his tail nice and high. "Of course we'll be here. Where else would we go?"

"We're both really excited to see what you'll be able to do next year. Aren't we, Mihku?" Sippy said. Mihku nodded and pranced across the garden to the marigolds, where he began digging a hole to store his nuts and berries for later.

"Yes, maybe our garden will be even bigger and better," he said, scrabbling through the dirt. "And let's add strawberries to the list for next summer, and sunflowers. I do love sunflower seeds."

"It will be," Kessa said, "and since we'll have more experience, we'll be better equipped to nurture it into a great patch of flourishing abundance." She swept her arm over the garden before her.

"Flourishing abundance?" Mihku chuckled. "That reminds me—Grandmother Woodchuck told us the meaning of your name. It means 'one who has a way with words.'"

"I like that. Tell her I think it's absolutely perfect." Kessa's eyes danced around the small patch of earth that, in two short months, had gone from weeds to bursting with ripe tomatoes and an abundance of fragrant herbs. She had never found a good way to stop Azeban from eating the plants, yet it seemed as though he had given up on his nightly pillages, because everything was growing with gusto. It had been a while since she had used her powers to revive any of the plants.

"Mihku? Did you ever end up asking Azeban to stay out of the garden?"

Mihku paused his furious digging for a moment and cocked his head to the side. "I did, but it didn't do any good. No, the reason he stopped destroying the garden was because he ran into a coyote. He kept coming back to try to steal more goods, but every night, the coyote would appear, even on the rainiest of nights. And there is no way Azeban is going to risk his life for some tasty basil and a few of our precious tomatoes, as good as they are. He's sneaky, but he's not stupid!"

Sippy pulled her beak out of a pecked-up strawberry and puffed out her chest. "I thought I saw a coyote around here too. He was lurking around yesterday, when you had that nice memorial for your poor old dog. We would have gotten closer, but we decided to play it safe up on your porch railing. I hope you don't mind we paid our respects from afar."

Kessa's heart swelled as she breathed the crisp morning air, taking in the increasing sparkle of the lake's surface. The plants had flourished after Bucky's death because he had returned to earth as a coyote and protected the garden and watched over it for them. That was the story she liked the best. Maybe it was the one she wrote, but one thing was for sure—somewhere, out over the Dawnland, the truth sailed along, just a handful of ashes carried by the wind.